For more than forty years,
Yearling has been the leading name
in classic and award-winning literature
for young readers.

Yearling books feature children's
favorite authors and characters,
providing dynamic stories of adventure,
humor, history, mystery, and fantasy.

Trust Yearling paperbacks to entertain,
inspire, and promote the love of reading
in all children.

OTHER YEARLING BOOKS YOU WILL ENJOY

Pure Dead
WICKED

Debi Gliori

A YEARLING BOOK

For Michael and Alex, who not only endured countless visits to StregaSchloss but also lit the candles and kept the fires burning. I owe you big.

Published by Yearling, an imprint of Random House Children's Books
a division of Random House, Inc., New York

ISBN-13: 978-0-440-41936-5
ISBN-10: 0-440-41936-0

Reprinted by arrangement with Alfred A. Knopf Books for Young Readers

Printed in the United States of America

August 2003

10 9 8 7 6 5 4

There are few, if any, maps on which the amateur orienteer might discover the coordinates for the village of Auchenlochtermuchty. This is because the indigenous population wish to avoid being overrun with tartan-liveried tour buses, tartan-tat tourist shops, and, in truth, tartan anything. The author respects the local population's desire to keep Auchenlochtermuchty's locus secret, and begs the reader to respect their wishes in maintaining it thus.

Contents

Dramatis Personae

THE FAMILY

TITUS STREGA-BORGIA—twelve-year-old hero

PANDORA STREGA-BORGIA—ten-year-old heroine

DAMP STREGA-BORGIA—their twenty-month-old sister

SIGNOR LUCIANO AND SIGNORA BACI STREGA-BORGIA—
parents of the above

STREGA-NONNA—great-great-great-great-great-great-
grandmother (cryogenically preserved) of Titus, Pandora, and Damp

THE GOOD HELP THAT WAS HARD TO FIND

MRS. FLORA MCLACHLAN—nanny to Titus, Pandora, and Damp

LATCH—butler

MARIE BAIN—cook, currently on holiday leave in Aix-en-Urtumiex

THE BEASTS

TARANTELLA—spider with attitude

SAB, FFUP, AND KNOT—mythical Schloss dungeon beasts

TOCK—crocodile inhabitant of Schloss moat

MULTITUDINA—rat, mother to multitudes, and Pandora's pet

TERMINUS—daughter of Multitudina

RESIDENTS OF AUCHENLOCHTERMUCHTY

MORTIMER FFORBES-CAMPBELL (Brigadier, ret'd)—hotel owner

FFION FFORBES-CAMPBELL—hotel manageress and wife of above

HUGH PYLUM-HAIGHT—roofing contractor, local businessman

VINCENT BELLA-VISTA—builder, demolition contractor, con man

VADETTE—fiancée of Vincent Bella-Vista

All resemblance to persons living or dead is unintentional, but the author wishes to acknowledge a growing similarity between herself and Tarantella and also to give thanks for the generosity of the International Institute for Advanced Witchcraft for permission to reprint one of their examination papers on the next page.

MASTER'S DEGREE EXAMINATION IN SORCERY & WITCHCRAFT

Paper IX (section C)

The events leading up to the Slaughter at Mhoire Ochone

Multiple Choice. One of the following statements is false.
Tick ONE option only.
Candidates will be disqualified for excessive ticks.

Question 42
Back in the time known as the Dark Ages, the indigenous dragon population of the Kyles of Mhoire Ochone were hunted for what properties?

A: Dragons had fire-breathing abilities and were thus sought after to provide drafty castles with a rudimentary form of central heating (q.v. the Frozen Buns of King James XIII).

B: Dragons laid eggs, which were the basis for the medieval Celtic Tourist Guild's claims re Loch Ness and all associated myths and legends pertaining thereto (q.v. *Leibendecker v. Scottish Tourist Board*).

C: Dragons were rumored to possess fabulous hoards of jewels and treasure, salted away in caves and roosts round Caledonia (q.v. *The Hobbit,* J. R. R. Tolkien).

D: Planting dragons' teeth in the ground and watering them was regarded as being the fastest method for creating a human army, short of conscription (q.v. *Jason and the Argonauts,* Homer).

E: The dragon's ability to fly made it a popular form of transport, handy for getting to Auchenlochtermuchty before last orders at the Quid's Inn (q.v. "Flight regulations for dragon pilots to be tightened up following incident over Lochnagargoyle," *Argyll Advertiser*).

F: As well as being an excellent source of phosphates, dragon diarrhea was much prized for its ability to dissolve unwanted intruders (q.v. *Pure Dead Magic,* Gliori).

From *The Annals of the Examination Board of the International Institute for Advanced Witchcraft* (April 1924)

Elementary Magic

Much later, Titus was to remark that this must have been the only time in history when a dirty diaper could be said to have saved several lives.

On that memorable morning, unaware of the terrible danger that hung over their heads, the Strega-Borgia family had been attempting to squash themselves into the interior of their long-suffering family car. Their shopping trip to the nearby village of Auchenlochtermuchty was long overdue, and consequently, all members of the family of two adults and three children were vociferous in their demands that they should not be left behind at home. Titus needed a computer magazine, Pandora had to buy something to eradicate a minuscule crop of pimples that had erupted on her chin, their baby sister, Damp, required more diapers, and their parents, Signor and Signora Strega-Borgia, had to go to the bank and do boring adult stuff.

As was usual with any planned expedition between

StregaSchloss and Auchenlochtermuchty, the process of leaving the house was taking longer than anticipated. Boots and coats had to be retrieved from the cloakroom, Damp had to be supplied with a clean diaper and given a ration of crackers to stave off starvation, and Titus needed to render himself deaf to everything going on around him by the simple expedient of clamping a pair of headphones round his head and pressing the PLAY button on his Walkman.

Titus threw himself into the car seat next to Damp, turned up the volume, and settled back with a smile. From outside the car, where she stood with her parents as they went through the ritual of finding checkbooks and car keys, Pandora noted with some satisfaction that Titus's expression was changing rapidly to one of disgust.

"PHWOARRR!" he bawled, competing with the deafening sounds inside his headphones. "DAMP! THAT'S DIS*GUS*TING!"

He struggled with his seat belt, desperate to put as much distance as possible between himself and Damp's odious diaper. Signor Strega-Borgia groaned, unbuckling his baby daughter and plucking her out of her car seat. Just at the precise moment that both Damp and Titus exited the car, the unthinkable happened.

A trio of vast and ancient roof slates that had clung to the topmost turret of StregaSchloss for six hundred years, held in place by little more than a clump of moss, broke free of their moorings and began their downward descent. Gathering momentum by the second, they barreled down the steep incline of the roof.

It all happened so quickly that initially the family were convinced that, for reasons unknown, an invisible bomber had dropped its payload directly onto their car. One minute they were standing around the unfortunate vehicle, happily slandering Damp's diaper, the next they were lying groaning on the rose-quartz drive, wondering what had hit them.

"What on earth?" Signor Strega-Borgia picked himself and Damp off the ground and ran to Signora Strega-Borgia to check that she was unharmed.

"Titus? Pan? Are you all right? Whatever happened?" Signora Strega-Borgia rubbed dirt off her clothes and stared at the car in disbelief.

"WHAT A WRECK!" yelled Titus, still muffled in his headphones. "LOOK AT IT! IT'S TOTALLY TRASH—*OWW!*"

"There," said Pandora with satisfaction. "That should help."

"Did you *have* to do that?" moaned Titus, holding his ears and glaring at his sister. His headphones dangled from Pandora's hands.

Signor Strega-Borgia was walking slowly round the wreckage of his car, surveying it from various angles, simultaneously horrified at the damage and amazed at the family's lucky escape. Embedded in the roof of the car, at a forty-five-degree angle to the battered paintwork, were three huge slabs of slate.

"We could all have been killed," said Signor Strega-Borgia reproachfully. He squinted up at the turreted roof of StregaSchloss, attempting to locate the origin of this attempt on his life. Beside him, Signora Strega-Borgia sighed. This was proving to be the most expensive morning's shopping thus far. To their list of items to be purchased in Auchenlochtermuchty, they now had to add one roof and one family car.

"We'll have to get it fixed," decided Signor Strega-Borgia.

le roof looks like it's in danger of raining down on heads."

The family automatically took several hasty steps backward, away from the danger zone. Titus tripped over a low stone wall and fell backward into a herbaceous border with a dismayed howl. Ignoring her son completely, Signora Strega-Borgia addressed her husband. "But that will cost a *fortune,* Luciano. Look, before we call in the experts, why don't you let me see if I can mend it. I'm sure there was something I learnt at college that would do the trick."

"Darling, I hardly think that your diploma in Primary Magic is a sufficient qualif—" He halted abruptly, alerted by the glacial expression crossing his wife's face.

Throwing her black pashmina dramatically across her shoulders, Signora Strega-Borgia stalked away from her husband across the rose quartz until she stood at the head of the steps leading down to the old croquet lawn. "I know you think I'm a half-baked witch, incapable, incompetent"—she choked back a sob—"inconsequential."

The front door opened and Mrs. Flora McLachlan, nanny to Titus, Pandora, and Damp, emerged into the December chill, shivering as she surveyed the family and their ex-car. "Now, dear," she admonished, gazing fondly at Signora Strega-Borgia, "there's no need to be like that. We all know that you're a very fine witch, indeed. . . ."

"Do we?" muttered Pandora.

"I don't *think* so," whispered Titus, crawling out of the herbaceous border and coming to stand next to his sister. Beside them, Signor Strega-Borgia sighed. If only Baci wasn't so *prickly*. He hadn't meant to insult her. Not really. Just perhaps to remind her that six months into a seven-year degree course in Advanced Magic might mean that her skills weren't exactly up to speed—yet.

"I'll prove you wrong," Signora Strega-Borgia promised, thrusting her arms wide apart and throwing back her head. Unfortunately this had the effect of making her look like a demented bat, and Titus had to avert his gaze to avoid bursting out laughing.

"My dear," said Mrs. McLachlan in alarm, "remember, if you would, that anger can cloud your judgment. Now let's not be too hasty. . . ." The nanny started down the steps toward her employer, but it was too late. Signora Strega-Borgia had already produced a small Disposawand from her handbag and was waving it erratically in front of her face.

"Healerum, Holerum . . . ," she began.

"Oh, no," sighed Pandora, "not *that* one."

"Stick . . ." Signora Strega-Borgia paused, racked her brain for the correct sequence of words, and continued undeterred, "Stickitum Quickitum, Renderum Fix."

There was a flash, a small apologetic puff of pink smoke, and the air was filled with the inappropriate smell of antiseptic cream.

"Oh, *dear*!" wailed Signora Strega-Borgia, covering her face with her hands.

"Oh, dear is right," groaned Titus.

"Oh, for heaven's sake, Baci. Just *don't* attempt to fix the car." Signor Strega-Borgia strode across the drive with Damp under one arm, stamped up the stairs into the house, and, seconds later, they all heard the sound of the bathroom door slamming shut.

Mrs. McLachlan, her mouth twitching with suppressed laughter, came over to where Signora Strega-Borgia stood hunched under her shawl, shoulders shaking, little sobs escaping from between her fingers.

"Och, pet," the nanny soothed, "it's not the end of the world. There's rain forecast for this afternoon, and that'll wash it off, and then we can call in a firm to mend the roof in a more . . . um . . . traditional fashion."

Signora Strega-Borgia peered out from between her fingers. "Oh, Flora," she wailed, "I'm useless. I mean, look at it. Look at what I've done."

At this moment, the sun chose to slide out from behind the clouds and spotlight the vast Band-Aid stuck to the topmost turret of StregaSchloss. The vision of eight hundred and sixty square feet of pink perforated plastic set against the gray slates of the roof was a little disquieting. With a wail, Signora Strega-Borgia ran for the house, her black shawl flapping behind in her wake.

"Oh, poor Mum," said Titus, horribly embarrassed by the sight of female tears. "I'd better go and see if I can cheer her up." He ran after his mother, leaving Pandora and Mrs. McLachlan gazing up at the bandaged roof.

"Can't *you* fix it?" said Pandora. "You know, with your amazing magic makeup case thing?"

The nanny immediately put her finger to her lips and made a shushing sound.

Pandora frowned and persisted. "Remember? Last summer?

You had that . . . that sort of transformer that changed . . ." She faltered. Mrs. McLachlan's expression was not even remotely encouraging. Moreover, the nanny's eyes had stopped twinkling. Pandora shivered. Suddenly she felt chilled to the bone.

"Heavens, is that the time?" Mrs. McLachlan gazed at her watch. "My fudge cake will be ready to come out of the oven in one minute. And you, young lady—not only are you appallingly inquisitive, you're also freezing cold. Come, child, inside with you." Taking Pandora's arm, she propelled her in the direction of the house. On the doorstep she paused and placed a gentle finger on Pandora's lips. "One: I can't fix the roof. Two: I don't have the makeup case anymore. Three: I swapped it for something better, and . . ."

"Four?" said Pandora hopefully.

"If I promise to tell you more when the time is right, would you please forget that we ever had this conversation?"

"Yes, I promise," said Pandora, bursting with unanswered questions, "but—"

"No buts," said Mrs. McLachlan in such a way as to indicate that not only was the subject closed, it was bolted, padlocked, and, in all probability, nailed shut.

With a thwarted snort, Pandora followed Mrs. McLachlan inside.

The Money Hum

From as far back as anyone could remember, there had always been somebody mending the roof at StregaSchloss. A succession of roofers with good heads for heights had clambered over its slates, scaled its pointy turrets, and once, memorably, poured hot lead over a particularly leaky section. This had caused the attic to burst into flames and initiated a temporary diaspora of several thousand attic-dwelling spiders.

Like the Forth Road Bridge, the roof at StregaSchloss was never finished. No sooner had one tribe of tradesmen vanished into the surrounding hills clutching a large check than another would appear, bearing scaffolding and slates, a stack of small newspapers with large headlines, and several tartan thermos flasks. Two days after the incident with the slipping slates, the Strega-Borgias braced themselves for the arrival of yet another firm of roofing contractors.

There was a pattern to this, Titus observed, stepping around a brimming soup tureen placed strategically under a leak from the cupola of the great hall. First of all, the roofers would arrive and consult with Mum. There would be much sucking in of air through teeth (the ferocity of the inhalation indicating how expensive the work was going to be). This would be followed by the traumatic discovery that none of their cell phones would work this far into the wilds of Argyll. Next came the erection of a web of rusty scaffolding; this was Titus's favorite stage, since his vocabulary of spectacular Anglo-Saxon curses had been garnered entirely from listening to these roofing tribes at work.

Titus practiced a few of these as his bare toes made contact with a particularly squelchy bit of rug in the great hall.

"I *heard* that," muttered Mrs. McLachlan, who came striding along the corridor from the kitchen. "I've lost Damp again," she said, "and I did hear the postman, but where's the post gone?"

A distant flushing sound followed by a cacophony of StregaSchloss plumbing alerted them both to Damp's whereabouts.

"FOR HEAVEN'S SAKE!" yelled Mrs. McLachlan. "DAMP! STOP IT!" And she shot along the corridor, expertly hurdling over brimming bowls and buckets in a futile attempt to divert the baby from her discovery that flush toilets can make all sorts of things disappear.

Titus ambled into the kitchen in search of breakfast. An alien reek of powerful aftershave assailed his nostrils. The source of this proved to be a balding man sprawled over the kitchen table across from Signora Strega-Borgia. Papers and glossy brochures were spread out amongst coffee cups and breakfast detritus. Titus's mother was frowning as she scribbled numbers on the back of an envelope.

Boring, thought Titus, scanning the shelves in the fridge. Yeuch, he amended, discovering a promising paper bag to be full of yellowing Brussels sprouts.

"Look at it this way, Mrs. Sega-Porsche," said the balding man, waving his coffee cup expansively. "It's like your dentist telling you that your teeth are fine but your gums have to come out. . . ."

"I'm not exactly sure that I understand," muttered Signora Strega-Borgia, frowning even more deeply and looking up from her envelope.

"Your coffee's wonderful, by the way," said Baldy, taking a slurp for emphasis, "best I've had for ages. . . . Anyway, your roof's fine. Great. Tip-top. Fantastic."

"And?" sighed Signora Strega-Borgia.

Titus found what he was looking for and slipped it into his pajama pocket.

"Excuse me, Mr. Pile-Um," said Signora Strega-Borgia.

"Pylum-Haight," interjected the bald man.

"*Indeed.*" Signora Strega-Borgia's voice developed a marked windchill factor. "Excuse me. Titus, put that back."

"Mu-ummm, just a wee drop."

"Put it *back*, Titus. I'm in no mood for an argument."

"But I want to see if it works," pleaded Titus, adding somewhat cuttingly, "None of your other spells ever do. . . ."

Signora Strega-Borgia stood up, sending brochures cascading to the kitchen floor. Titus sighed and handed her a small glass vial. Signora Strega-Borgia sat down again and flashed her visitor a patently insincere smile as she placed the vial on the table in front of her.

Mr. Pylum-Haight could read the label on the side of the vial, magnified through the glass of the coffeepot.

Tincture of Ffup-tooth
to be diluted x 10
5 ml equivalent to 1 Battalion

Mentally logging this knowledge under Weird Things Clients Keep in Their Fridges, Mr. Pylum-Haight pressed on. "As I was saying, your roof is in great shape, but the beams supporting it . . ."—pause to suck in dramatic lungfuls of air—"rotten to the core, 'm'fraid. In fact, you're really lucky the whole thing hasn't collapsed on you, what with all the rain we've been having. . . ." Meeting Signora Strega-Borgia's steely glare, he faltered and took a deep draft of chilly coffee to sustain himself.

"So . . . Mr. Pylum-Haight . . . what exactly *are* we talking about?" Signora Strega-Borgia folded her calculation-laden envelope into a small parcel and pushed it to one side.

Titus sat at the other end of the kitchen table and waited. Now, he guessed, was not the time to raise the question of an increase in pocket money in line with inflation.

"A rough estimate—ballpark figure, off the top of my head, can't be too definite about this, not set in stone, but possibly in the region of, give or take a few . . . um . . ."

"*How much?*" insisted Signora Strega-Borgia.

Pylum-Haight hastily scribbled a figure on the back of a business card and stood up. "Have a wee think," he advised. "It's a big job. Expensive business keeping on top of these old houses. I know several clients who would be willing to take it off your hands. Get yourself something more manageable. More modern. Maybe your husband might like to give me a ring to discuss . . ." His voice trailed off as he busied himself with folding and packing the tableful of brochures and papers back into his crocodile-skin attaché case. "Nice to . . . um . . . Thanks for the . . . er . . . We'll be in touch," he muttered, sidling in the direction of the kitchen door. "See myself out . . . um . . . Thanks again." And he tiptoed backward out into the corridor, leaving a trail of aftershave behind him.

Titus listened to the sound of footsteps fade into silence. The front door creaked open and, seconds later, slammed shut. Over the faint ticking of the kitchen clock came the sound of a car engine, a crunch of gravel under tires, and the valedictory honk as Tock the moat-guarding crocodile bid the parting guest farewell.

"Mum?"

"Not right now, Titus," mumbled Signora Strega-Borgia, waving a hand absently around her head, as if to ward off a fly. She gazed at the business card in front of her as if it might be coated with plague bacteria. "I need to find your dad." She reluctantly picked up the card and rose to her feet like a sleepwalker.

"He's upstairs mending my modem," said Titus. "Mum—what's the matter? I'm sorry I made that comment about your spells. I didn't mean it."

Signora Strega-Borgia turned, her face pale and drawn. "It's not your attack on my skills as a witch, Titus. No, it's nothing"—she glanced hastily at the card in her hand—"nothing that six hundred and eighty-six thousand, eight hundred and seventy-five pounds, seventy-two p plus VAT won't fix."

The kitchen door closed behind her as Titus was left staring bleakly at the tabletop in front of him. Picking up a discarded brochure and his mother's pencil, he calculated that, at his current rate of pocket money, it would take him a mere three and a half millennia to acquire that kind of sum. The brochure showed a picture of an ideal family in front of their new home. There were a dog, a cat, a baby, and two grinning children flanked by their smiling parents. The new home behind them was built on a model that a five-year-old might draw: a front door, one window on each side, three windows above, and a perfect leak-free roof on top. The blurb read: "The Buccleuch family at home in Bogginview. Homes to depend on. Homes to raise your family in. BOGGINVIEW. Another quality build from BELLA-VISTA DEVELOPMENTS INC. . . ."

Not even remotely like *our* house, thought Titus. If they'd decided to make a brochure about StregaSchloss, we'd be scowling on the moth-eaten croquet lawn: "The Strega-Borgias at home with their dragon, their yeti, their griffin, and . . . oh, yes, their moat-guarding crocodile. Behind them, you can just see their modest little STREGASCHLOSS, which looks like a cross between a fairy castle and the film set for *Vlad the Vampire Falls on Hard Times*. . . ."

Titus threw the brochure back on the table and stalked out of the kitchen. And I just *bet* that the Buccleuch fridge is full of pizzas and chocolate fudge cake, instead of moldy Brussels sprouts, he decided, skirting an overflowing chamber pot on his way upstairs. No wonder they're grinning, he concluded.

Beasts in the Bedchamber

Life at StregaSchloss had its drawbacks. For a start, it was three miles to the nearest village, and when you finally cycled there, down rutted lanes and puddles that could have hidden a small submarine, you wondered why you'd bothered. Auchenlochtermuchty boasted three public bars, one hotel, four banks, one shop that called itself a hardware emporium, selling everything from hoof picks to garden forks, and one mini-market that never had what you needed but stocked heaps of things that you didn't.

No swimming pool, thought Titus, no cinema, no sweetshop. . . . Gloomily, he pushed open his bedroom door. The curtains were drawn and the room was in total darkness. Fumbling his way toward the window, Titus flung open the drapes and gazed out at the nearby sea-loch. Last night's snow was beginning to melt in the rain. A small cough from behind him alerted Titus to the fact that he was not alone. He spun round and shrieked, "What on earth d'you think you're playing at? Get out of there! Off my bed, you filthy beasts!"

From underneath Titus's duvet, the ancient eyes of Sab the griffin, Knot the yeti, and Ffup the teenage dragon regarded him with little interest. Plucking boredly at the pillow with a long black talon, Ffup addressed the wall: "Chill out, Titus," he drawled.

"WHAAAT?" said Titus.

"The dungeon's flooded, which means we're allowed upstairs till it dries out, the kitchen has your mum and a perfumed Suit in it, the library fire's gone out, and this place seemed like a good idea. You're supposed to cherish us, right? We're the low-tech security system at StregaSchloss, remember? You got a problem with that?"

Confronted with the impossibility of forcibly evicting the three massive beasts, Titus backed down. "But my bed," he moaned. "*Look* at it. It's all bent out of shape, and it's soaking."

The beasts ignored him. Knot scratched vigorously in his clotted fur, causing the bed to quiver ominously beneath him.

"I'm *freezing,*" complained Sab. "My paws are like lumps of ice."

"Consider them thawed." Ffup sat up, drew back his massive head, and, with a giant snort, fired twin blasts of flame from his nostrils.

"NO! AAAARGH! MY BED!" wailed Titus.

"Whoops, silly me," the dragon said, as the bedpost caught fire. "Knot, don't just lie there scratching; *do* something."

Silently, the yeti stood up in bed and leaned toward the flaming bedpost. Stretching out his woolly wet arms, he engulfed the burning timber in a damp, hairy embrace. With a loud hiss, the fire went out. Titus's bedroom filled with the unappetizing smell of burnt, damp old dog. Downstairs, the front doorbell rang.

With the family car out of action, Pandora had retrieved her rusty bicycle from the depths of the potting shed and spent two days attempting to render it roadworthy. Bouncing down the rutted track to Auchenlochtermuchty in the rain had dampened her enthusiasm for shopping, and the combination of discovering that her bicycle had developed a flat tire and that the village shops were devoid of cosmetic cures for erupting pimples had done little to raise Pandora's spirits. By the time she had pushed her bicycle back to StregaSchloss, she was utterly fed up. She gazed unseeing at the familiar turrets reflected in the moat, and when Tock raised his scaly snout from its icy depths and gave his usual honk by way of hello, she barely responded. Leaning on the doorbell, she watched as Tock levered himself out of the water and waddled toward her, baring his many yellow teeth in a crocodile greeting. This kind of sociable behavior sent postmen and delivery boys running for cover, but Pandora knew the crocodile to be an ardent convert to vegetarianism, and she reached down to pat his head.

"What're you doing out of your moat? Honestly, sometimes I think we take our policy of cherishing our beasts too far. Other people make their crocodiles into handbags and shoes, while we extend them an unconditional welcome." Pandora pressed the doorbell again and called through the letterbox, "Come on, open the door, I'm turning into a human icicle out here."

"Nnnngbrrr," agreed Tock, adding hopefully, "Hot bath? Steamy tiles? Fluffy towels?"

"Yes, but I'm not exactly sure that Mum would approve," said Pandora. Besides, she decided, if anyone needed the hot bath and fluffy towels, it was her.

The front door opened and Tock bolted inside.

"Oh, not *another* one," groaned Titus, stepping aside to let his sister in. "I just found Sab, Knot, and Ffup dripping all over my bed. Where does Tock think he's going?"

The sound of Schloss plumbing in full bath-pouring din drowned Pandora's reply.

The Tincture Topples

So close to midwinter, darkness fell at StregaSchloss around three o'clock with an almost audible thud. The wind began to gather momentum, peppering the windows with rain and causing the house's fifty-six chimneys to resonate in a manner that was both eerie and mournful. Clustered round an enormous log fire in the library, the clan Strega-Borgia were not inclined to be cheerful.

"I'm *freezing,*" moaned Pandora for the umpteenth time.

"Put another log on, then." Titus barely glanced up from his laptop.

"For heaven's sake," groaned Signora Strega-Borgia, muffled in mohair blankets, pashminas, serapes, sheepskin slippers, and woolly gloves, "we're supposed to be economizing. D'you think that stuff grows on trees?"

The library door opened and Mrs. McLachlan entered, balancing a tea tray on one hip as she herded Damp into the room.

"Careful, dear," she warned the baby. "Mind the fire. HOT HOT BURRRRRNY."

"*Not,*" muttered Pandora, huddling closer to the flames and nudging Tock with her toes. "Move over, you brute, you're hogging all the heat."

The crocodile ignored her, inching closer to the fire in a determined search for warmth.

"Now then." Mrs. McLachlan propped the tea tray on a fireside table and peered into the depths of the teapot. "Bearing in mind that we're all a bit down in the dumps today, I've made some scones, a fruitcake, some lemon drench cake, and a few wee meringues, just to tide you all over till suppertime. . . ."

Damp beamed up at her nanny in absolute adoration. Since Flora Morag Fionn Mhairi ben McLachlan-Morangie-Fiddach's arrival at StregaSchloss the previous summer, the baby had fallen deeply in love with her baking, her lullabies, and her comforting pillowy chest.

Titus brightened at the thought of all that food and abandoned his laptop in favor of calories.

"What a pig," muttered Pandora, trampled underfoot by her brother in his haste to be first with the meringues. "Look at him, Dad," she said disgustedly. "He always grabs the biggest one before anyone else has a chance."

Signor Strega-Borgia looked up from the pages of his book. "Oh, Lord," he sighed, gazing up at the ceiling, "was that a drip? On the back of my neck?"

"No, Dad." Pandora cut herself a modest sliver of fruitcake and put it on a plate. "The drip's sitting beside you, stuffing its face with meringues."

"Dripshh don't haff fashes," Titus said indistinctly, swallowing hard and helping himself to seconds. "Mind you"—he stared at his sister—"neither do you. You've got pimples. Lots of them."

"That's ENOUGH!" yelled Signor Strega-Borgia. "Be quiet, both of you, and listen. . . ."

From the room above came a faint percussive sound, a rhythmic *plink plunk plink*. Signora Strega-Borgia shivered and drew her blanket closer round her shoulders. The tapping grew louder, more insistent, faster . . . *plink-plunk, plink-plunk, plinkplinkplink, plunk*.

"I'm going upstairs to see what's going on." Signor Strega-Borgia stood up and promptly tripped over the slumbering Tock. He fell to the floor with a crash as a large chunk of plaster dropped off the ceiling and embedded itself in the chair he'd recently vacated. The descent of the plaster was followed by a deluge of cold brown water, pouring down through the hole in the cornice and soaking the furniture beneath.

"Oh, NO!" wailed Titus. "My laptop!" And he dived to rescue it from the flood.

"Typical." Pandora rose to her feet and glared at her brother. "Not 'Oh-Dad-are-you-all-right-gosh-that-was-a-lucky-escape,' but 'Oh-laptop-oh-heavens-what-a-near-miss.' "

"I think we ought to continue this discussion somewhere else, don't you, dear?" said Mrs. McLachlan, hoisting Damp into her arms and handing Titus the dish of meringues. "And perhaps you'd like to carry these to the kitchen?" Her voice brooked no argument. "And, Pandora, could you manage the tea tray with the rest . . . ?"

"QUICK! OUT! NOW!" yelled Signor Strega-Borgia, pushing Mrs. McLachlan and Damp toward the door. "The whole ceiling's about to come down."

Signora Strega-Borgia shot to her feet, shook the sleeping crocodile awake, and hurried to the door in a tide of cashmere. Above her head, a vast gray patch spread like ink on blotting paper across the damaged ceiling. Around the newly created hole a bulge began to develop, growing and sagging as if something massive were pressing into the library from the room above. With all his family safe in the hallway, Signor Strega-Borgia shut the library door. From behind it came a rending crash followed by the deafening roar of gallons of pent-up rainwater pouring through a large hole.

Latch, the Schloss butler, appeared on the landing above. He was dressed informally since he'd been enjoying a rare afternoon off duty, and consequently was sporting an alarmingly small green dressing gown, from which his long limbs sprouted like pale potato shoots.

"There appears to be some problem with the roof," he said redundantly, since the sound of water pouring into the library could clearly be heard through the closed door. "Can I be of some assistance? Phone a plumber? Fetch more buckets? Sandbags? Try to salvage some books from the library . . . ?"

Pandora noticed that water was beginning to seep into the hallway from under the door.

"Phone Pylum-Haight," said Signor Strega-Borgia.

His wife flinched. "But, Luciano . . . ," she whimpered. "The expense . . ."

"I'm sure we can come to some arrangement with Mr.

Pylum-Haight." Signor Strega-Borgia wrapped an arm round his wife. "Let's not worry about that right now, shall we? And, Latch: if you'd give me a hand taking the books down to the kitchen to dry out? Later—when the floods have stopped?"

"Oh, the books—the poor *books,*" wailed Signora Strega-Borgia, realizing the full extent of the damage. "My magic books, the children's picture books . . . the family books. . . ." She began to cry, her head buried in her husband's shoulder.

"Now, dear—don't you fret about that right now," Mrs. McLachlan soothed. "A nice cup of tea in the kitchen, with a wee dram for the shock." She shifted a wide-eyed Damp to her other hip and took her employer by the arm to lead her downstairs.

Their voices faded away as the nanny led Signora Strega-Borgia toward the kitchen. The door closed, muffling any further discussion. Tock gave a mournful honk and waddled off in the direction of his mistress's bedchamber.

Two hours later, a rusty white van and a sleek black BMW were parked outside the front door, and a tribe of men in yellow oilskins headed by Mr. Pylum-Haight had invaded StregaSchloss. Books adorned every available surface in the kitchen. Soggy paperbacks, drenched calfskin, and pulpy wet hardbacks dripped in every nook and cranny. The family sat round the kitchen table, their spirits lightened somewhat by Mrs. McLachlan's carrot and ginger soup, roast chicken, potatoes and broccoli, and Sussex Pond Pudding. The room was warm, the children full and sleepy. From overhead came the sound of banging and hammering as

Pylum-Haight and his emergency team effected a temporary roof repair.

"The roof appears to be far worse than we'd suspected. Mr. Pylum-Haight was being horribly gloomy about how long he thought the work would take, not to mention how much it would cost. . . ." Signora Strega-Borgia sighed and pushed her plate away.

"He says we can stay here tonight," said Signor Strega-Borgia, watching in amazement as Titus spooned out a fourth helping of pudding onto his plate, "but tomorrow we have to move out."

"But Christmas is only three weeks away," moaned Pandora, curled up in an armchair by the range.

"And where are we going to move out *to*?" Titus had paused with his spoon arrested in midair. "We don't *have* another house."

"We don't even have *this* one right now," said Signor Strega-Borgia gloomily.

"We could use my tent," said Pandora. "Or rent a caravan. . . ."

"NOT!" bawled Ffup. "If you think I'm sleeping under canvas in December, you can think again." The dragon banged on the table for emphasis and glared at the assembled company.

No one noticed as a small glass vial bounced off the tabletop and smashed on the stone floor below. No one noticed as its contents spilled out and seeped into the cracks in the floor. Oblivious to the appalling chain of events unleashed by his teenage tantrum, Ffup carried on: "And how exactly d'you think *I* am supposed to cope with being cooped up in a tin box? Caravan? *Phtui* . . . I spit on it."

Mrs. McLachlan fixed the dragon with her basilisk stare. "Ffup . . . ," she warned.

The dragon blushed pink and seemed to shrink inside his scaly carapace. "Um . . . yes," he bleated. "Caravans . . . mmm, *lovely*. What *fun*. Come to think of it, I rather like tinned humans, actually. . . ."

Full-on Vadette

The hour was way past midnight when Mr. Pylum-Haight drove across StregaSchloss's uninhabited moat and edged his BMW through the open gates and out along the pitted drive that wound back to Auchenlochtermuchty. Pylum-Haight lit a foul-smelling cigarillo and sank back into the black leather of his seat. He pressed a keypad on the dashboard and the display on his car phone promptly lit up. A muted dial tone began to trickle from all eight of the concealed speakers in his car. "Come on, pick up, pick up," he said, exhaling a mouthful of evil brown smoke that temporarily obliterated the reek of aftershave clinging to his person.

The dial tone stopped, and a woman's voice spoke. "Bella-Vista residence, Vadette speaking."

Not *Vadette,* groaned Pylum-Haight to himself. Oh, please let her develop instant laryngitis. . . . Bracing himself, he replied, "Hello, love. Is the man himself around? It's Hugh—Hugh Pylum-Haight."

On the other end of the line, he could hear the rattle of ice cubes as someone took a large gulp of their drink. "Oh, it's you, Huey . . . ," came the reply. "*Huey*. Wee Huey. Now, why don't you just bog off, wee man, and phone the office instead? Vincent is not available to take calls tonight."

"Look, love . . ." Pylum-Haight discovered that he'd chewed the end off his cigarillo in an effort not to scream out loud, hurl his car phone out the window, and drive straight into the nearest available tree. "I know it's late, but I've got to have a word with Vinnie. Something urgent's come up."

Another rattle of ice cubes. "What? What's up, Huey? Why don't you tell *me*, and if *I* think it's important enough, then I'll let him know. . . ." *Clink, chink, rattle.*

Breathing deeply, Pylum-Haight swerved round a corner and almost succeeded in avoiding a particularly deep pothole. "Vadette, pet, I don't think you need bother your vacant—sorry, your *pretty* head about this. Just tell the man to come to the phone—*please,*" he begged.

Clink, tinkle, glug.

Vadette appeared to consider this for as long as it took for whatever she was drinking to slide down her throat and then, with no warning whatsoever, she screamed, "VINNIE! It's that WEE POSER again!"

"Aaargh, my *ears,*" moaned Pylum-Haight, deafened by the eightfold onslaught of Vad-the-Mad at full throttle.

"Yer what? That you, Huey? What's the problem? It had better be important—I'm missing the darts." In the background came a roar of applause and a voice calling, "One hundred and *eighty*!"

"I'll be brief, Vinnie." Pylum-Haight slowed to a crawl behind a police patrol car that had nosed out into the road ahead. "It's that site you had your eye on—you know, the big old castle by the lochside—"

He was interrupted by Vinnie yelling, "Leave it out, Vadette, would you? Stop dancing in front of the screen—I can't see the *game.*"

Pylum-Haight rolled his eyes. He could imagine the scene in Vincent's hilltop house. The vision of Vadette obscuring the picture on Vincent's wide-screen television as she gyrated and wobbled in front of it was the stuff of which nightmares were made. Poor Vincent, he thought, such appalling taste in girlfriends.

"Come and sit on my lap, then, that's a good girl."

Pylum-Haight choked on his cigarillo, and tried to turn it into a cough. Sit on his lap? Vincent would be asphyxiated—Vadette must weigh . . . a hundred and fifty kilos? Two hundred?

"That house with the weird name?"

Vincent was evidently still breathing. Pylum-Haight failed to imagine how. "The same," he said. "But I think it might just be about to fall into your lap. . . ."

There was a loud thump and a wail from the other end. He must have dropped her onto the floor, Pylum-Haight thought in amazement.

"Are you straight-shooting, Huey?" Vinnie's voice was harder now, closer, as if his mouth was pressed up close to the eight car speakers.

"Cross my heart, Vinnie. By the new year, I'll have done so much damage to the roof I can guarantee that the present owners will be desperate to sell StregaSchloss to Bella-Vista Developments Inc. In short, to you."

"Five hundred chalets . . . ," the voice murmured reverently, as if Vinnie were running his hands through priceless gems. A thousand caravans, leisure complex, bowling alley, games arcade; knock down that boring old castle, build a multistoried car park. . . ."

"Don't forget the fish farm *and* the nuclear power station," added Pylum-Haight. "And the abattoir, the rendering plant, and the animal research facility. . . ."

Perfectly Beastly

The prospect of a removal from StregaSchloss, however temporary, would have given the most seasoned team of movers pause for thought. Not so the Strega-Borgias, who threw themselves into the effort with gusto. Even baby Damp caught the general mood and packed all her teddies for removal from the house. She pulled on the Disappearing Handle, all the better to dispatch them quickly, but to her disappointment, the Magical Vanishing Thing (better known as the downstairs toilet) failed to make her teddies dematerialize. Instead, back they came, soggy of fur and plush, bringing with them an assortment of drenched envelopes and a mushy wodge of old toilet paper. Puzzled, Damp staggered off in search of a Grownup.

"There you are, pet." Mrs. McLachlan looked up from packing nursery essentials into a large wooden crate. She took in Damp's wet and disheveled appearance and gave a deep groan.

Plucking the baby off the floor, she bore her off to the bathroom. "How many times do I have to tell you? Toilets are dirty. DIRTY. DIRRRTY."

Damp gazed at her wet hands. They looked clean enough to her. She hesitated, then popped a comforting thumb back in her mouth.

"NO! DON'T DO THAT!" Mrs. McLachlan shrieked. "TAKE THAT OUT OF YOUR MOUTH *NOW*!"

In the kitchen, Titus choked on a mouthful of last night's meringue. Such was his ingrained obedience to the nanny that he spat the contents of his mouth back onto his plate.

"Puh-leeaze," groaned Pandora. "Spare me. I *know* you're gross—you don't have to keep on proving it to me."

In the great hall, boxes and trunks lay in stacks, some with their contents spilling across the flagstones, others tightly bound and chained with huge padlocks. Signora Strega-Borgia muttered to herself as she added rusty keys to a hoop hanging from her waist. Her husband was deep in conversation on the telephone, one hand cupped over his ear in an attempt to hear the voice at the other end.

"Now, let me see . . . ," mumbled Signora Strega-Borgia. "All the grimoires are packed in the old sea trunk. The flasks of hen bane are in cotton wadding in the lead-lined casket—the isinglass decanted into those thermoses. . . ."

"Shall we begin again?" Signor Strega-Borgia rolled his eyes in impatience. "I'd like to book *four* rooms and your stables, *not* four tables, and for the rest of the month, through to the new year."

". . . my wands and cauldron are in the pink hatbox, ceremonial pointy hat in the black hatbox, candles, incense, and ectoplasm in that string bag over there—blast, the ectoplasm's escaped. . . ."

"Not four *kennels*, no. All your stables. . . . Yes. . . . Ah—I thought you might ask me that. . . . Not *dogs*, no. . . . Nope, not horses, either. . . . Um, well, I suppose you have to know sometime. . . . Actually, what we're talking about is a crocodile, a griffin, a yeti, and a very small and terribly well-behaved dragon. . . ."

"KNOT!" bawled the dragon, crashing through the front door. "YOU HORRIBLE, FOUL, DISGUSTING, SNOT-ENCRUSTED HEATHEN!"

"Where *has* that ectoplasm slithered off to?" Signora Strega-Borgia muttered in the background.

"Could you keep it *down*, for Pete's sake," hissed Signor Strega-Borgia, returning to his phone call. "Sorry about all the racket. . . . No, no, it was the roofing contractor, not one of our *pets*—heavens, no."

"WHAT D'YOU CALL *THIS*?" The enraged dragon extended a claw from which dangled a vast amorphous blob of dirty green jelly.

" 'S NOT MY FAULT," called Knot from the doorway of the dining room. He shuffled downstairs to examine the fascinating substance adhering to Ffup's claw. "Never seen it before," the yeti decided, patting it with a matted, hairy paw. "Looks pretty tasty, though," he added, beginning to drool.

The dragon shuddered. "WOULD SOMEONE GET THIS GIANT BOGEY OFF ME?" he bawled.

"My pleasure," said Knot, stepping forward.

"No . . . no, STOP!" shrieked Signora Strega-Borgia. "My *ectoplasm*!"

Knot licked around the gap in his clotted fur that functioned as a mouth. "Mmm*hmm*. Oh. Sorry. . . . D'you want me to see if I can get it back?"

"Great," said Signor Strega-Borgia bitterly. He replaced the receiver in its cradle and turned to glare at Ffup and Knot. "You two have just added another zero onto the end of our hotel bill."

"What hotel?" said the dragon belligerently. "What bill? Nobody mentioned anything about a hotel to *me*. No one ever tells *me* anything."

" 'S not fair," added Knot.

"One of these days you two will realize that the whole world doesn't revolve around you—in the meantime, *we* are going to live at the Auchenlochtermuchty Arms while the roof here is mended." Signor Strega-Borgia smiled. "And you beasts are booked into the adjoining stables, hot and cold running slops and as much straw as you can eat—"

"WHAAAAAT?" Sab, the griffin, staggered downstairs from Titus's bedroom, his leathery forelegs piled high with clothes. "But I thought you'd booked us a suite," he complained. "You know—white towels, free shower caps, en suite tea and coffee—that sort of thing."

Tock appeared at the front door with a carrier bag full of lily pads from the moat clamped between his jaws. He deposited these on the doorstep and pointed behind himself with an extended claw. "Taxis are all here."

Bumping slowly down the drive came a fleet of black cabs,

one for each beast and a spare for the family, Mrs. McLachlan, Tock, and Latch.

Panic ensued. Suddenly, the great hall filled with flying dust, shouts and screams, loud crashes as cabin trunks were slid hastily downstairs, and the resultant wails as they made painful contact with shins. Suitcases and bags multiplied until the hall looked like a baggage claim, but then, miraculously, ten minutes later, everything had vanished into the interiors of the waiting taxis. The family, staff, and beasts stood shivering on the steps of StregaSchloss.

"I'm sure I've forgotten something important." Signora Strega-Borgia climbed with difficulty into an overloaded taxi. Tock leapt in behind her, his bag of lily pads dripping in his wake.

"Your son, perhaps?" inquired Signor Strega-Borgia, snapping the clasps shut on a computer packed into an aluminum flight case and handing it through the taxi window.

"Titus!" called Pandora. "Don't worry—you'd *hate* it anyway. May as well stay put."

Mrs. McLachlan, halfway into the bulging interior of the taxi, turned round and shot her a look.

"Sorry, I just couldn't help myself," Pandora said, walking back into the great hall.

"COME ON, TITUS!" she yelled. "Get your rear in gear—we're going. NOW!"

"Coming," came a faint voice from the depths of the house.

Pandora folded her arms and waited. The great hall already had an air of abandonment about it. The carpet had been rolled up and put away for safekeeping, along with vast paintings, suits of armor, and rusting shields that had adorned the walls of StregaSchloss for as long as Pandora could remember. The grandfather clock, shrouded in dust sheets, and the crystal chandelier hanging over the stairs were all that remained. The hall echoed to the sound of approaching footsteps. Titus appeared at the end of the corridor leading to the kitchen. Pandora noted that his hands were clutching several laden cake boxes.

Seeing her expression, he explained. "Seemed a shame to leave all this food for the rats. . . ." His voice trailed off weakly.

"Multitudina!" wailed Pandora. "I've forgotten her! *And* Terminus—oh, no! I must find them. . . ."

"They're *rats,* Pandora. You can't take rats to a hotel—anyway, they've probably got millions of their own."

Outside, the taxi sounded its horn. Pandora was stricken. My pet rat, she thought, stifling a small sob. And her daughter. Abandoned. Alone in an empty StregaSchloss.

Seeing his sister's eyes fill with tears, Titus relented. "We can come back, Pan. Don't panic. Rats can look after themselves, and we can keep on popping in with food for them." He patted her awkwardly on the back, dropping a cake box as he did so. Its lid fell off, and a large scone rolled out and bowled along the hall floor. "There," he said. "That'll keep them going for *ages*. Now come on, we have to go."

Propelling his sister outside, Titus pushed her toward the taxi and then returned to close the front door. With a mournful groan of rusty hinges, it slammed shut behind him.

Terminus Undone

Silence descended on StregaSchloss. Dust began to settle in the great hall, eddying and swirling in the drafts blowing down through the hastily mended library ceiling. A tap dripped in the kitchen sink and a clock on the mantelpiece slowly wound down. Below it, in the firebox of the range, coals turned from red to ashy gray. Degree by degree, the temperature dropped as StregaSchloss went into hibernation.

In her nest of shredded newspaper in the pantry, Multitudina, the free-range rat, snored faintly. Curled between her mother's front paws, Terminus opened one yellow eye and pulled Multitudina's whiskers. Hard.

"Ow!" squeaked Multitudina. "What was that for?"

"Hungry," muttered Terminus. "Bigger snacks, *now*."

"Heavens, child," said Multitudina, struggling to her feet and gazing at her fuzzy pink offspring with dislike, "you've a lot to learn about manners. What's the magic word? P—p—p—?" she prompted.

The ratlet raked her mother with an incredulous stare and yawned. "Want it," she stated baldly. "Food. Now."

Multitudina sighed. Never, never, never again, she vowed for the hundredth time. No more babies, ever. "You're big enough to look after yourself," she growled at her daughter. "Don't lie there demanding room service. Show some independence. Have you ever thought of finding a place of your own? I'll help you pack," she added hopefully.

Terminus ignored this. Her nose twitched. She could smell something. Something edible. Throwing caution to the wind, she ran out of the pantry and found herself in the wide-open spaces of the kitchen floor. The kitchen table towered above her, its four huge legs leading up to unimaginable heights, its checked tablecloth draped . . . just . . . within . . . reach.

Swinging wildly on a corner, Terminus slowly clawed her way upward, paw over paw, claws digging into the loosely woven fabric. Inelegantly, she dragged herself onto the tabletop like an exhausted swimmer emerging from the deep end of a pool. For a while, she lay beached and panting on the tablecloth, then her greed reasserted itself. She stood on her hind legs and surveyed the kitchen from the vantage of the high tabletop plateau, mentally logging the fact that the tablecloth was strewn with little bread boulders, puddles of cow juice, and little smears of bee-sticky. Unable to resist the opportunity, she climbed onto the rim of an abandoned milk jug and yelled in the direction of the pantry, "Yoo-hoo, O wrinkly one! Bet you're too old, fat, and smelly to catch me before I eat this lot!"

From high above the ratlet's head, a husky voice drawled, "I have to agree. Your mother is indeed way too crumpled, ancient, and odiferous to halt you in mid-glut, but *I'm* not."

And before Terminus could turn her head to discover the source of this boast, something the size of a tennis ball dropped down from the ceiling and drop-kicked her into the milk jug.

The ratlet came up for air, thrashing and choking, milky bubbles inflating on the end of her nose, her whiskers dripping white. Through a film of milk, Terminus peered up to the rim of the jug. What she saw was not reassuring. Silhouetted against the light with two hairy legs dangling down into the depths of the jug was a giant spider. A spider with a distinctly menacing attitude. A spider that was, for the time being, ignoring Terminus's attempts to escape the milk bath and appeared to be combing her copious body hair with a small comb made out of bone.

"Attractive, isn't it?" observed Tarantella, twiddling the comb idly, turning it over and over all the better to admire it. "If memory serves me correctly, I think it used to belong to a relative of yours . . . um, was it your father? Brother? Great-aunt? *Yes,* that was it. It was your great-aunt Indiscretiona's. Her left femur, I believe. . . ."

Just before Terminus fainted in sheer terror, she saw the spider bend down toward her, its mouthparts coming closer and closer until the ratlet's entire field of vision was filled with pink. The last thought that passed through her head as she slid beneath the surface of the milk was that for some perverse reason, the spider appeared to be wearing lipstick.

Since her intention had not been to harm Terminus, just to put the frighteners on her, Tarantella draped the unconscious rat-baby over the edge of the milk jug and sauntered off in search of something more appetizing.

Compliments to the Chef

The girl behind the reception desk at the Auchenlochtermuchty Arms appeared to be slightly stunned by the arrival of the entourage from StregaSchloss. Her brief experience of the hotel trade had failed to prepare her for the odd assortment of guests and luggage attempting to negotiate the revolving door at the hotel's main entrance. Towed by Tock on a chain, Pandora skidded across the marble floor and fetched up under an antique chaise longue. The revolving door slowed to a more sedate pace and Mrs. McLachlan stepped into the hotel with Damp, a handbag, and Sab on a tight leash.

"Sit, boy," she commanded, flashing the receptionist a brief smile and gently lowering Damp to the floor.

"What's this *sit* nonsense?" demanded the griffin under his breath. "What d'you think I am—a *dog*?"

"Good afternoon," Mrs. McLachlan addressed the receptionist. "We're part of the Strega-Borgia party. I believe you have some rooms booked in that name. . . ."

"What PARTY?" screeched Ffup, barging through the revolving door, his chain clanking behind him. "No one told *me* there was going to be a party."

". . . So if you could just tell me where our rooms are," continued Mrs. McLachlan serenely, "and where I might find the stable block for the animals . . . ?"

The receptionist had turned deathly pale and slumped over her desk, scattering pens and ledgers as she did so. Sensing that all was not going well, Mrs. McLachlan turned round in time to see Tock ambling across the tartan carpeting, dragging his dripping bag of lily pads behind him as he smiled a wide and toothsome greeting at the receptionist. Through the revolving door came Titus, Latch, and Signora Strega-Borgia, loudly informing anyone within earshot that Knot was outside in the parking lot being copiously sick.

"Dis*gus*ting," said Signora Strega-Borgia, holding something infinitely unpleasant at arm's length. "But at least I got it back. Oh, Latch, be a *dear,* would you, and give this a bit of a rinse?"

The butler twitched slightly, but obediently took hold of the regurgitated ectoplasm and bore it off to a bathroom.

Exactly one half-hour later, the family, minus Knot, reconvened in the dining room, immensely cheered by the discovery that the Auchenlochtermuchty Arms had indeed earned its four-star reputation. The family had variously bounced on the beds, peered into the mini-bars, turned on the televisions, and channel-surfed, and even Damp had spent a happy twenty minutes ironing her teddy bears flat in the trouser press thoughtfully supplied by the management.

After some heated discussions, Pandora was sharing a room with Mrs. McLachlan, Titus with Latch, and Signor and Signora Strega-Borgia installed a travel cot for Damp at the end of their bed and sighed mightily at the prospect of sharing a room with their early-waking baby. Mollified by the thought of lunch, the beasts and Tock obediently unpacked in the stables, left Knot groaning on a heap of clean straw, and joined the family round a linen-clad table by a window in the dining room.

The clan Strega-Borgia settled in their chairs and began to decipher their leatherbound menus. Mrs. McLachlan tucked a linen napkin under Damp's chins and began to translate the menu for the benefit of those who couldn't read. "Now Tock, dear, here's a nice vegetarian dish just for you: fricassee of wild mushrooms with rice—or perhaps the salad of baby artichokes on a bed of lamb's lettuce. And Titus?" she prompted. "What would you like, dear?"

Titus scanned the menu. What *was* all this stuff? he wondered. His eyes alighted on something that looked vaguely familiar. "Steak tartarr," he pronounced with a confidence that he didn't feel, "with poms freet."

Pandora scowled behind her menu. Trust Titus to order first, she thought. Not to be outdone, she added, "And *I'll* have the huevos rancheros with guacamole." There, she decided, that'll put his gas at a peep.

"Isn't guacamole the stuff that seagulls cover rocks in?" asked Titus.

"That's *guano,*" sighed Mrs. McLachlan, "and it's very impolite to talk about such things when we're about to eat, dear."

A waitress appeared holding a large carafe of ice water and two bread baskets. She placed these in the middle of the table, produced a notebook and pencil from her pocket, and laboriously began to take the family's order.

The fireplace clock measured out ten minutes while the Strega-Borgia tribe waited patiently, nibbling on bread and sipping ice water in happy anticipation of the feast to come. Ten more minutes ticked by, and then a further ten, by which time the bread baskets were empty, the water carafe drained, and tempers beginning to fray. Damp had quickly tired of playing peekaboo with her napkin and had begun to grizzle; Titus was whistling tunelessly through his teeth and drumming on the tablecloth with his fork in time with some internal rhythm of his own; and Pandora was attempting to glean some measurement of entertainment from re-reading the menu.

"I wonder what has happened to our lunch?" said Latch.

Hiss hiss, tappety tap. Hiss.

"I'm *starving,*" moaned Pandora, looking up from her seventeenth tour of the menu.

Tap, tappety, hiss, tap-tap.

"This is ridiculous," muttered Signor Strega-Borgia. "Much longer and it will be time for *supper,* not lunch."

Hiss. Tappety tap, hiss hiss.

"Oh do shut *up,* Titus," snapped Pandora. "*Stop* that. You're driving me insane."

"What?" squawked Titus. "What have I done *now*? Stop what?" He glared at his sister. "You're always so grumpy when you haven't eaten," he added. "Actually, cancel that: you're *always* grumpy, period."

Just as the family was about to erupt in preprandial hostilities, the waitress reappeared with a laden tray from which she began to serve lunch.

"Mmm, lovely," lied Mrs. McLachlan, cutting Damp's shriveled fish into baby-sized bits and somewhat redundantly blowing on them.

"What is *that*?" hissed Titus, prodding the red mush that oozed blood across his plate. "It's not even *cooked*," he complained.

"Quit moaning," said Pandora, seizing the opportunity for revenge. "You're always so grumpy when you haven't eaten." She took a vast forkful of her lunch and swallowed it without noticing the many small flecks of jalapeño pepper that garnished her plate. She was so hungry that she managed to devour five more mouthfuls before the full effect of the chilies struck her.

"I'm not eating *raw* meat," said Titus, pushing his plate in Sab's direction.

The griffin frowned at the blood-stained steak that was Titus's rejected lunch. "What d'you think it was?" he said, poking it with a talon and adding darkly, "Or *who*, for that matter?"

Pandora's eyes watered, her throat closed up, and her tongue announced its intention of spontaneously self-combusting. "Wa . . . te . . . r . . . ," she croaked, seized by a chili-induced coughing fit.

"Give it five seconds with both nostrils," advised Sab, passing Titus's lunch over to Ffup.

The waitress returned with another water carafe in time to witness Ffup aiming a blast of dragon fire onto Titus's raw steak. Ffup misfired and the bread baskets burst into flames.

"For heaven's sake!" yelled Signor Strega-Borgia, leaping to his feet just as the tablecloth caught fire. Unaccustomed to dealing with guests who were attempting to flame-grill their own food, the waitress flung the contents of the water carafe at the burning tablecloth and fled to the kitchen. Drenched in icy water and picking up on the general mood, Damp began to sob.

"Good Lord," came a woman's voice, "the chilies weren't *that* hot." Bearing down on the remains of the Strega-Borgia's table was an overdressed woman carrying a fire extinguisher. She pointed its nozzle at the table and sprayed everything in sight with foam. The Strega-Borgias regarded the blackened ruins of their lunch in dismay. In the interval of stunned silence that followed, Pandora decided that she loathed this woman on sight. Clad from head to toe in a clinging jumpsuit made from real zebra skin, the wielder of the fire extinguisher smiled a cold little welcome and adjusted her fox-fur collar in such a fashion that the glassy eyes of the deceased mammal fixed their accusing gaze on the floor.

"I need some fresh air," whispered Pandora, sidling out of the dining room before she was sick over the woman's crocodile-skin shoes. Running into the hall, she saw that the young Tock-phobic receptionist had been replaced by a middle-aged man who was too engrossed in pouring himself a drink from a flower vase to pay any attention to her hasty flight upstairs. From the dining room came a mocking peal of laughter and the ringing tones of a woman's voice caroling, "Oh, she's your *daughter,* is she? What a funny little thing she is. And *what* a handsome crocodile. *Lovely* skin. . . ."

Pandora, eyes, throat, and now face aflame, fled for the shelter of her bedroom.

Something's Cooking

Despite the smoke damage in the dining room, business at the Auchenlochtermuchty Arms carried on as usual. The disgraced beasts and Tock were relegated to the stable block and Signor and Signora Strega-Borgia installed themselves on the sofas in the residents' lounge. Mrs. McLachlan and Damp explored the gardens in the company of Latch while Titus and Pandora discovered the true meaning of boredom.

In the bedroom she shared with Mrs. McLachlan, Pandora sat glassy-eyed in front of the television while Titus crawled under her bed in search of a telephone socket into which he could plug his laptop and access the Internet. He retreated backward from under the bed, muttering, "Right—surf's up," and logged on. Beeping sounds came from the laptop as it dialed out to an ISP located somewhere in deepest Argyll. Waiting for the connection to establish itself, Titus idly chewed his fingernails, gazed unseeingly out of the window, and wished with all his heart that he could return to StregaSchloss.

I've only been here for twenty-four hours and already I'm bored, he thought. Bored, bored, bored. At least at home I could go and raid the fridge, but I'm not allowed to do that here.

In front of him, a dialogue box informed him that he was now connected to the Net. The cursor blinked on and off, politely waiting for Titus to enter an address. Without hesitation, he typed:

www.diy-clones.com

pressed ENTER, and then sat back again to wait for the interminable time it usually took to gain access to the Web site.

The previous summer, Titus had accidentally stumbled on this address when he mis-keyed in the name of his favorite ice cream manufacturers. He'd been starving after dinner, and after a fruitless trawl of the freezers for ice cream, he had decided to see if he could set up a direct supply of Dairy Cones to StregaSchloss. Diy-clones had been the result of his hasty typing, and after he'd spent five gripping minutes exploring the many attractions of that fascinating Web site, Titus had completely forgotten how hungry he was. Now, six months later, in an upstairs bedroom of the Auchenlochtermuchty Arms, he was inching closer to making a major scientific breakthrough. The screen on his laptop glowed deep red as the Web site came online. Titus logged in his password, bypassed screenfuls of introductory stuff, scrolled rapidly through pages of mathematical calculations, and arrived at what he was looking for. There. It all seemed simple enough. All he needed was:

fresh blood
some growth medium

an incubator
and an infrared facility.

Checking a side panel on his laptop, he found that he had at least one of the requirements at hand. His computer had the ability to communicate data by means of an infrared transmitter located next to the modem input. But as to where he was going to find the rest of his list . . . Titus sighed. Fresh blood was going to be a bit tricky, not to mention totally gruesome. He could just about manage to acquire some of his own—if he shut his eyes and stabbed himself with a badge pin, he was sure he could squeeze out enough blood for his needs before he fainted.

Pandora's blood was another matter entirely. Titus eyed his sister speculatively, wondering how to go about this without simultaneously causing her too much pain and alerting her to what he was doing. For the time being, he was reluctant to let Pandora in on his master plan for creating two clones, one of himself and the other of her, mainly because if he shared the secret with her, he would also have to inform her that he needed her blood. It was unlikely that she would see the scientific necessity for this. However, he mused, Pandora would be the first to agree that creating clones for the purpose of doing homework (Pandora-type clones) and tidying the bedroom (Titus-type clones) was a stroke of utter genius. Staring through Pandora as his thoughts turned this way and that, he realized that she had turned the television off and was gazing at him in alarm.

"Titus . . . ?" She shivered. "What *is* it? You're looking at me very strangely . . . almost as if you've turned into a—a *zombie* or something."

Titus snapped out of his reverie and grinned wolfishly at her. "Not a zombie, sister *dear*. A vampire, actually. . . ."

He'd worked out how to do it, he realized. In fact, Pandora had worked it out for him. Fresh blood was going to be easy. Now he could turn his attention to the two remaining items on his list.

"What are you doing?" said Pandora, peering over his shoulder before he had time to log off from the incriminating Web site. "Is that *another* game? *Diy-clones*? Don't you just hate it when people spell things wrong on purpose? Die doesn't have a 'y' in it."

"Um, yes," Titus mumbled, barely listening as he frantically tried to leave the Web site without Pandora catching a glimpse of anything that might alter her assumption that he was playing yet another *Death & Destruction* type of computer game. Distraction was the only answer, he thought, as he saw her squinch up her eyes and try to read what was written on the screen on his laptop. Distraction, plus a little bit of laying the foundations for his newly hatched plan to acquire some of her blood. . . .

Titus took a deep breath. "Pan . . . ," he began, leaning backward on Mrs. McLachlan's bed in a manner more designed to obscure his sister's view of the computer than to afford him any comfort, "d'you think I look a bit pale?" Titus opened his eyes a little wider and sneaked a quick glance at Pandora to see how this was going down.

"Nope. Not even slightly," she stated. "In fact, you're blushing."

"Um, no, I meant—d'you think I'm looking a bit flushed?" Titus hastily amended. "Running a temperature kind of thing?"

Pandora gave up trying to read Titus's screen and stood up. "Titus, what *are* you on about?"

"It's just that I'm a bit worried . . . ," Titus improvised. "Last night I—it was awful—I woke up and found myself lying on the stairs—I don't know how—not the foggiest idea of how I got there."

"You were probably sleepwalking," Pandora said, delivering this statement in the uninterested tone of a weather forecaster predicting icy spells in January.

Delighted that Pandora had swallowed this fictional hook without any difficulty, Titus pressed home his point. "But . . . I could do *anything*—end up *anywhere* when I'm sleepwalking . . . and I wouldn't be able to do anything about it. I wouldn't even *remember* what I'd done."

Pandora rolled her eyes and exhaled noisily. "I wouldn't let that worry you, Titus. You *never* remember what you've done. You've got the cognitive capacity of a goldfish. If you were a computer, you'd crash as soon as anyone switched you on—"

"WHAT?" roared Titus. "I've got a memory like an *elephant*!"

"No, Titus." Pandora opened the bedroom door and stepped out into the corridor. "Your memory isn't like an elephant's. Just your appetite."

The door slammed shut behind her.

Quid Pro Quo

Two weeks dragged slowly by. The Strega-Borgia hotel bill swelled into an alarming five-figure sum, much to the dismay of Signor and Signora Strega-Borgia. Over breakfast, Signor Strega-Borgia waded his way through a sheaf of slips, commenting bitterly on each one as around him the family tried to eat breakfast as inexpensively as possible.

"How on earth did we manage to run up a phone bill for four hundred and eighty-three pounds ninety-six?" Signor Strega-Borgia waved the offending item at his wife, who wisely declined to answer.

Titus, recalling his hours spent on the Internet, failed to quell the blush advancing across his cheeks.

"We've only been here for sixteen days," moaned Signor Strega-Borgia to the array of bent heads across the table. "Look at this—laundry facilities: two hundred and ninety-five pounds plus VAT—we could *buy* a washing machine for less. . . . And here—room service: eight hundred and thirty-seven pounds, forty-two—that's *ludicrous*!"

Signora Strega-Borgia looked up from her toast. "That'll be the food for the beasts, darling—"

"What have they been eating, for heaven's sake? Beluga caviar? Lobster thermidor? Wild boar and truffles?"

Signora Strega-Borgia ignored the interruptions. "Since they're not allowed in the dining room anymore, the poor dears do need their creature comforts."

"SUNDRIES!" bawled Signor Strega-Borgia, spotting another attempt to plunder the family's diminishing finances. "Look—one linen tablecloth: three hundred and ninety pounds; ten linen napkins: a hundred and fifty pounds; two bread baskets: fifteen pounds forty; damage to table: two hundred and ninety-three pounds—"

"Good morning. Is everything in order?"

Signor Strega-Borgia started guiltily. The hotel manageress, Mrs. Fforbes-Campbell, had appeared as if on oiled wheels beside the table and was fixing upon the family a smile that was remarkable only for its lack of sincerity. Her hooded eyes told a different story altogether.

Pandora's cereal spoon clattered into her bowl, bounced out across the tablecloth, and catapulted its milk-sodden contents straight onto the manageress's left shoe. Pandora gave a small squeak of dismay, inwardly logging another item onto the day's bill—one pink ostrich-skin shoe: two hundred pounds. She gritted her teeth and decided not to apologize—the ghastly woman was a walking advertisement for humanity's history of cruelty to animals: her shirt was the product of overworked silkworms, her rabbit's-foot brooch a gross reminder that somewhere out there was a bunny amputee limping across the heather, and her suede skirt had cost some innocent sheep dear. Why, then, Pandora wondered, was Dad being so *chummy* with her? She clenched her fists as a loud peal of laughter rang out across the dining room.

"Oh, Luciano," Mrs. Fforbes-Campbell shrieked, "you're such a scream!"

"Indeed," muttered Signora Strega-Borgia, raising her coffee cup and her eyebrows in tandem. "Could I have some more coffee, *Mrs*. Fforbes-Campbell?"

Uh-oh, thought Pandora, registering the chill in her mother's voice.

"Certainly, Signora," said the manageress. "I'll just make some fresh . . . myself, I never drink the stuff—so bad for the complexion."

One all, thought Pandora, dreading what she knew from experience was to come.

"Personally," said Signora Strega-Borgia to no one in particular, "I rely on our impeccable genetic heritage to look after my complexion." She smiled to herself and idly smoothed a stray hair back into place, looking up to deliver the final thrust straight between Mrs. Fforbes-Campbell's eyes. "You will discover in the fullness of time that good breeding *always* wins hands down over mere diet and artifice."

Game, set, and match, thought Pandora, restraining a desire to stand on the tabletop and cheer.

Apparently embarrassed by this catty interchange, Mrs. McLachlan had taken refuge behind her powder compact, peering into its oval mirror and tutting as she made ineffectual little dabs at her nose with a tiny sugar-pink puff. Latch sighed and buttered another slice of toast. Personally, he thought, Flora McLachlan had no need for such lily-gilding. The boss was absolutely right: good genes knocked spots off paint and powder. . . .

Something in the nanny's mirror had displeased her, though—displeased her mightily—for Mrs. McLachlan snapped her compact shut, hurled it into her handbag, and stood up abruptly, shooting Mrs. Fforbes-Campbell the look that Latch had privately defined as "The Hairy Eyeball." She hoisted Damp out of her high chair, scrubbed porridge off the baby's cheek with a napkin, and turned to Signora Strega-Borgia. "If you have no objections, madam, I thought I would take the girls into the village for a spot of Christmas shopping."

"Good idea," agreed Signora Strega-Borgia, "and Titus . . . ?"

"Pandora, dear, run and fetch your coat and we'll meet you at the front door." Mrs. McLachlan smiled at Titus. "I haven't asked you to join us because I know you've done your shopping already."

"I did mine online," Titus said with unbearable smugness. "So much easier. Avoid the crush and rush. No parcels to carry. No old ladies spearing you with their umbrellas. No grumpy crowds on the streets, no cheesy Santas in grotty grottoes. . . ."

Vaguely comprehending that her favorite icon was being unjustly slandered, Damp gave a small squeak.

"No, dear," agreed Mrs. McLachlan. "Though I hardly think

downtown Auchenlochtermuchty can compete with the horrors of Christmas shopping on Oxford Street, but I'm sure that you're right." Clutching her handbag, Mrs. McLachlan bore Damp off upstairs to dress her for the excursion.

On their way through the hotel grounds ten minutes later, Mrs. McLachlan and Pandora saw Latch taking the beasts out for their morning exercise. Tock bolted across the vast manicured lawn, his webbed claws leaving a trail of prints on the white frosted grass. The crocodile halted under a skeletal oak and began to dig frenetically with all four paws. Silver frost turned to green grass and then to dark earth as Tock clawed downward.

Assuming incorrectly that this was standard procedure for reptiles about to off-load the previous night's dinner, Mrs. McLachlan's party strolled on past the earthworks. They failed to grasp the significance of the black armband tied round one of Tock's front legs. By the time they reached the main road, they were too far away to notice Tock pause in his labors, reverently place a small brown leathery object in the recently dug hole, and then begin to fill it back in again.

Auchenlochtermuchty was not given to extravagant flights of Christmas decorations. Strung across the main street were some rather haphazardly spaced strings of colored lightbulbs, and in the window of the hardware store, a tatty sign blinked a myopic greeting of M   Y C RI TMAS. Each of the four banks had posters displayed in their windows encouraging passersby to MAKE THIS CHRISTMAS ONE TO REMEMBER, if only for the level of debt incurred. The mini-market demonstrated that the rogue apostrophe was alive and well in Auchenlochtermuchty, with banners offering FREE-RANGE TURKEY'S, FINE WINE'S, and, oddly, FRESH ASPARAGU'S.

And a Merry Christma's to you, too, thought Pandora, pushing open the door of the shop in order to admit Mrs. McLachlan and Damp in her stroller.

Two hours later, they had finished. The parcel tray on the stroller sagged under the weight of stripey carrier bags from the mini-market and the packages from the hardware shop. Mrs. McLachlan decided that lunch was overdue and led her charges into the lounge bar of the Quid's Inn. They settled in a battered leather snug and, after a brief consultation, ordered two chickens with fries and a bowl of tomato soup for Damp. The baby had fallen asleep and now lay sprawled across her stroller, pink-cheeked and snoring faintly. Mrs. McLachlan and Pandora happily examined their purchases, comparing notes on the suitability or otherwise of their various gifts.

"What on earth is that thing?" Mrs. McLachlan held a tiny bundle of string and twigs up to the light, turning it around, trying to work out what it might be for.

"The man in the hardware store said that it was a spider ladder. Here—let me." Pandora unfolded the bundle, which did, indeed, reveal itself to be a miniature ladder, complete with tiny wooden rungs. "I thought Tarantella might find it useful for hoisting herself out of baths. I couldn't find anything for Tock, though, could you?"

Mrs. McLachlan dug deep in a stripey carrier bag and produced a trio of plastic bath ducks.

"Perfect!" said Pandora, unwrapping one of her brown-paper packages. "And look what I found for Knot."

Mrs. McLachlan peered at the bottle in Pandora's hands. " 'Organic hair detangling conditioner,' " she read. "What a good idea—that yeti's fur defies every hairbrush ever invented. . . . What's that, dear?"

"It's a 'Handy Motorist's Fire Extinguisher,' " said Pandora, reading the product label. " 'For boat or caravan use,' " she quoted, adding, "Also handy in expensive hotels for extinguishing tablecloths."

"That'll be for Ffup, I take it," said Mrs. McLachlan. "Oh, look, here comes our lunch."

They repacked their purchases and sat back in their seats while a waitress slid two laden platefuls of chicken and fries onto the table. "Salt 'n' sauce? Ketchup? Vinegar? Mayonnaise?" she inquired.

"Yes, please," said Pandora and Mrs. McLachlan in unison.

The waitress disappeared and returned immediately with all five condiments, a pile of paper napkins, and a bowl of tomato soup for Damp.

"This is so much nicer than the hotel," said Pandora through a mouthful of fries. "I really don't like that Mrs. Fforbes-Campbell and I know she doesn't like us much."

Mrs. McLachlan stopped chewing and looked Pandora straight in the eye. "On the contrary, dear," she said, dabbing at her lips with her napkin, "Mrs. Fforbes-Campbell is *unusually* fond of your father."

"Yeuchhh," said Pandora. "She's way too old for him, and besides, he's *married*. To Mum."

"Mrs. Fforbes-Campbell is also married," said Mrs. McLachlan, "but she's not the kind of woman to let a little thing like wedding vows stand in her way. Mark my words, dear, that woman is *trouble*. She intends to do her level best—" Mrs. McLachlan suddenly stopped in mid-prediction, conscious that she'd said far too much already. Bending her head, she applied herself to her plate as if her life depended on it.

"How come you know so much about her?" Pandora's brows knitted themselves into paired question marks. "Can you read minds or something?"

"Mmm . . ." Mrs. McLachlan sought refuge in a cloud of vagueness, hoping that Pandora would drop the subject.

This was not to be. "Come on, Mrs. McLachlan, prove it," challenged Pandora. She put her cutlery down on her plate, closed her eyes, and concentrated. "Right, I'm thinking about something now—if you can really read minds, then tell me what's in mine."

"Pandora, stop being silly—your lunch is getting cold."

"I'm *concentrating,*" said Pandora. "Surely that makes it easier for you."

"Don't be daft, dear. . . ."

Conscious that Mrs. McLachlan was weakening, Pandora smiled. Her eyes were still tightly shut.

"Oh, very *well,*" Mrs. McLachlan sighed, pulling out her powder compact from her handbag, "but you must keep your eyes closed." She lifted the compact's lid and peered inside.

Black as pitch, the tiny mirror began to undergo a subtle transformation. Its surface bubbled like boiling toffee, turning dark brown, then bronze, and finally clearing to a beautiful transparent gold. Below the mirror, the face powder swirled as if there were a hidden undertow running below its surface. At the very instant an image formed in the mirror, the face powder halted in its tidal motion and threw up the words:

WHAT A PIG YOU ARE, CHILD

Mrs. McLachlan stifled a laugh as she realized that this referred to the mirrored image of Pandora eating a vast slab of Banoffee Pie, the current dessert on the Quid's Inn lunchtime menu. She looked up and found Pandora staring at her.

"I peeked," Pandora confessed. "Sorry, I just couldn't resist. So: what was I thinking about and, more importantly, what is that in your hands? Is this what you meant when you wouldn't tell me your secret the day Mum Band-Aided the roof?"

Mrs. McLachlan rolled her eyes in despair. Glancing in her compact before she closed its lid, she caught a glimpse of a Pandora-shaped cat with all four paws in the air, and written in the powder was the observation:

. . . AND SUCH A NOSY ONE, TOO

"In answer to your impertinent questions, your mind *was* full of Banoffee Pie, but *now,* dear, you're feeling a wee bit ashamed. Curiosity killed the cat . . . ?"

"Meow," whispered Pandora in as apologetic a tone as she could muster. "But, Mrs. McLachlan, what *is* it?"

The nanny passed the object across the table to Pandora. "Its official name is the soul mirror, but the manufacturers prefer us to call it the i'mat."

"Is this what you swapped your makeup case for?" Pandora peered at the golden compact, admiring the intricate filigree engraved on its surface.

"Sort of." Mrs. McLachlan smiled but didn't volunteer any more information as to its provenance. Pandora held the i'mat gingerly in the palm of her hand. "Don't worry," Mrs. McLachlan continued, "it won't bite you, and unlike my makeup case, you can't actually use it to *change* anything; it's really just for *seeing* things. . . ."

Pandora was only half-listening. The compact lay in her hand, surprisingly heavy for such a small object. Something about its weight, its sheer presence, made her wary. Sensing this, Mrs. McLachlan leaned across and opened it for her. "Go on," she said. "Try it out. See what Damp is dreaming of."

Carefully, as if it might detonate in her hand, Pandora pointed the compact at her baby sister. Instantly, the mirror turned to gold and the powder popped out the incomprehensible message:

NUM NUM NUMM

"*What*?" Pandora squeaked. "What on earth . . . ?" Tinted with gold, the mirrored image was of a huge breast. "For heaven's sake, Damp, what *is* this?" Pandora groaned, not understanding at all. In the mirror, a tiny winged Damp clamped herself to the breast with a beatific smile.

"Eughhh. GROSS," Pandora gagged. "I'm *never* going to have babies when I grow up."

The powder in the compact shuffled to form the single word:

YUM

Snapping the compact shut, Pandora returned it to its owner. Damp stirred in her stroller, her lashes fluttered, and she awoke. In front of her, a bowl of tomato soup steamed invitingly. Trying to reconcile the food of her dreams with the hot soupiness of reality was too much for the baby. When Mrs. McLachlan dipped a spoon in the bowl and offered it to her, Damp took one look, opened her mouth, and burst into tears.

Despite Mrs. McLachlan's best efforts, Damp was still sobbing when they arrived back at the hotel. Signora Strega-Borgia was having an afternoon nap, and Pandora found her father in the residents' lounge helping Mrs. Fforbes-Campbell trim the Christmas tree. To Pandora's disgust, Mrs. Fforbes-Campbell had turned this innocent activity into an opportunity for close physical contact with Signor Strega-Borgia. To wit: "Luciano, be a *darling* and pass me up that glass angel—oh, I'm *so* sorry, I simply can't reach, you'll have to come up the ladder here beside me. . . ." and: "Can I just pass this garland over your shoulder like *so* . . . ?"

At this tender moment, Pandora announced her arrival by jumping onto a box of decorations. "Oh, heck! What *have* I done? Gosh, sorry—I hope it wasn't too valuable?" Glancing upward as she delivered this patently insincere apology, Pandora distinguished her father's look of utter relief as he disentangled himself from Mrs. Fforbes-Campbell's garlandy embrace as well as the manageress's slitty-eyed gaze of utter loathing.

Signor Strega-Borgia descended the ladder and wrapped an arm round Pandora's shoulders. "Let's go and wake Mum up, shall we?"

"With a kiss," said Pandora, smiling fixedly up to where Mrs. Fforbes-Campbell perched, stranded in a tangle of abandoned greenery, looking for all the world like the Wicked Fairy in a geriatric version of *Sleeping Beauty*.

Beastly Behavior

Mortimer Fforbes-Campbell (Brigadier ret'd) sprayed gray fluff out of an aerosol can onto a crate of bottles of inferior Bulgarian red. Earlier that day, he'd removed all the wine labels and replaced them with some that he'd had printed specially for the evening's festivities. The labels he'd removed had proclaimed the contents of the bottles to be TANNIN UT TRANSYLVANIA and sported a rather jolly illustration of a Bulgarian housepainter steeping his brushes in a vat of T ut T. Whether this was a warning or a recommendation was hard to tell, but the new labels re-identified the wine as RIOJA DE TOROMERDE. The tasting notes printed on the little label on the reverse of the bottle read, "Aged in oak stalls, this wine has been described as Old Spain's most famous export."

Since *Toromerde* translates literally as "bull excrement," the label was being disarmingly truthful. Mortimer, in a state of total ignorance of the meaning of any language other than

English, was blissfully unaware of what the new wine labels signified. All he knew was that he could get away with charging more for Spanish Rioja than Transylvanian Brush Restorer. He finished spraying gray fluff over the bottles and stood back to admire his efforts.

"Top-hole, what?" he addressed his wife, who was busy decanting a vat of jaded calamari into a series of microwave dishes. "Pile 'em high, sell 'em dear, don'tcha know, old girl?"

"*Did* you invite Hugh?" Mrs. Fforbes-Campbell picked out a decomposing specimen of shellfish, sniffed it, and dropped it into the waste disposal.

"Who?" barked Mortimer, disappointed at his wife's lack of interest in his endeavors.

"For God's sake, Morty, turn your hearing aid on. *HUGH:* DID. YOU. INVITE. HUGH. PYLUM-HAIGHT?" she bawled.

"Never heard of the fellow. Sounds foreign. Ghastly chaps, foreigners. That bally Italian bunch we've booked over Christmas. Keep on whingeing about the size of their bill. Chap's a bit too chummy with you, what?"

"Not chummy enough," muttered Mrs. Fforbes-Campbell, sliding a batch of calamari into the irradiation unit and switching it on. A ghostly blue light played over the rancid shellfish, rendering them bacteria-free but regrettably still well past their sell-by date.

"Whatcha say, old thing?" Morty struggled upstairs with two crates of seemingly venerable, dusty bottles of vintage Rioja.

"I SAID, 'HAVE. WE. GOT. ENOUGH,' " Mrs. Fforbes-Campbell yelled, adding under her breath, "Moron."

Mortimer's reply was lost as the buzzer went off on the irradiator. Mrs. Fforbes-Campbell removed the first batch of steaming squid and slid the next trayful in. Checking that her husband was well out of earshot, she picked up the phone and dialed Hugh Pylum-Haight's private number. "Darling," she said in her most seductive whisper, "it's me. . . ."

That night, the Auchenlochtermuchty Arms was hosting a Christmas Eve Wine-Tasting Event that rashly promised to BANISH THOSE WINTER BLUES WITH A MEDITERRANEAN NIGHT TO REMEMBER. GO ON—YOU DESERVE IT. And all for a mere twenty-five pounds per head. In a rare fit of financial madness induced by a total lack of ideas for what to give as Christmas presents, Signor Strega-Borgia had decided that not only did he deserve such a treat, but so, too, did his wife, nanny, and butler. This largesse was extended to the beasts and Tock, all of whom were vastly cheered at the prospect of a night in the hotel instead of the dank and depressing stable block. Permission for their re-entry into the Auchenlochtermuchty Arms had been sought from Mrs. Fforbes-Campbell and grudgingly granted with the proviso that this was a one-time-only indulgence and that after Christmas, the beasts would go back to being barred.

Consequently, freshly washed and pressed, the beasts were the first guests to arrive in the cocktail lounge. Dressed in an off-the-shoulder flamenco dancer's dress made of red chamois leather, Mrs. Fforbes-Campbell greeted them in a less-than-effusive fashion. "I suppose you'll be wanting a drink . . . ?"

Sab took charge. "I'll have lemonade, Knot had better not, and Tock? Ffup?"

Catching sight of the platters of irradiated squid, Tock slid the contents of one down his throat, belched tactfully, and turned his attention to the bottles ranged behind the bar. "Make mine a Gatorade," he said, propping one scaly elbow on the bar rail and attempting to exude urban sophistication.

"I suppose you don't do Dragonade," sighed Ffup, helping himself to a shriveled peanut and turning round to stare at the door as several more guests arrived. A small Latin man in a deafeningly loud check suit limped up to the bar and kissed Mrs. Fforbes-Campbell's outstretched hand.

"Darling boy," she trilled, air-kissing him near both cheeks. "Vincent, how *lovely* to see you . . . both." The last word was delivered with a disappointed sneer, for Vincent Bella-Vista was accompanied by his girlfriend, Vadette, who was advancing on the bar with all the subtlety of an armored tank.

"Sweetie," Mrs. Fforbes-Campbell hissed at Vadette, "don't you look just *stunning*? Haven't you lost some weight? Doesn't she look super, Vincent?"

"Spare me, Fifi," muttered Vadette, plonking her considerable girth onto a bar stool. "Just pour the drinks."

"*Not* Fifi, darling—I'm not a poodle."

"Fee-Yawn, then. Pour the gut rot, there's a good dog."

Just in time to avert an all-out catfight, a brash of visiting American lawyers on vacation arrived at the bar. Their search for signs of the Loch Ness Monster in Lochnagargoyle's chilly depths had drawn a blank, but they were cheered at the prospect of suing the Scottish Tourist Board for misinformation regarding the possible existence of the fabled Nessie. Their combined girths made Vadette look positively svelte, and their voices, trained in the law courts of Carolina, drowned out any further discussion.

"Some of your wine for my learned colleagues at the bar," their spokesman demanded, "and make mine a double Scotch on the rocks." The speaker drummed tanned fingers on the countertop, jiggled loose change in his pockets, and gazed around. "Say, ma'am," he drawled in some puzzlement after encountering the combined stares of the beasts and Tock, "did we get our wires crossed? Is this Fancy Dress Night?" He stepped forward and peered at Tock with interest. "Say, feller," he said admiringly, "that's a pretty darn realistic costume you've got there. How much did that ole 'gator skin set you back?"

Tock opened his mouth to reply. The combination of his squid-tainted breath and his serried rows of teeth made the American recoil sharply. "Well, Bud"—Tock attempted a mid-Atlantic accent—"it's not what ya know, it's *who* ya know. My mom was in the skin trade, if you follow my drift."

The door of the cocktail lounge opened to admit Hugh Pylum-Haight, wreathed in cigar smoke and dressed in an impeccably tailored dark cashmere suit. He elbowed his way to the bar and tapped Vincent Bella-Vista on the shoulder. Looking like an aristocrat and his gamekeeper, the two men moved away to a secluded corner and were soon deep in conversation. Beelzebub, the resident cat of the Auchenlochtermuchty Arms, was curled up in the fireplace, attempting to ignore the unwelcome attentions of Knot, who persisted in sniffing the cat's fur and drooling in a most repulsive fashion. The smell of cigars mingled with wood smoke and, outside the windows, snow fell. The lounge was full to overflowing by the time the Strega-Borgia party finally appeared.

The room fell silent as all eyes beheld Signora Strega-Borgia. Dressed in a simple green velvet sheath with her black hair falling glossily over one shoulder, she looked like a mermaid. Her lack of makeup or jewelry only served to accentuate her natural beauty. The crush of bodies parted to allow this vision access to the bar. Signor Strega-Borgia, Latch, and Mrs. McLachlan followed in her wake. Around them, interrupted conversations were resumed and a measure of normality returned to the lounge.

Mortimer, on bar duty, goggled, choked, and managed a smile halfway between a leer and a grimace.

"Luciano? A glass of wine? Latch? A hot toddy for your cold? Flora?" Signora Strega-Borgia smiled at Morty. It was the kind of smile mermaids use to lure sailors onto rocks. Morty floundered. His hands shook as he uncorked a wine of his relabeled gut rot. Signora Strega-Borgia reached out and took the wine from his trembling hands. Reading the label, she began to laugh. "I don't believe it," she said, passing the bottle to her husband. "Mr. Fforbes-Campbell—is this some kind of joke?"

Signora Strega-Borgia failed to notice the manageress bearing down on her, lips drawn back in a snarl, eyes flashing danger. Pretending to catch her stiletto heel in a crack in the floorboards, Mrs. Fforbes-Campbell staggered into Signora Strega-Borgia with a girlish shriek of dismay. "Oh, my *dear*!" she gushed, recovering her balance, "your *poor* dress. Oh, heavens above, and red wine, too. Awful. So sorry. Only one thing for it. . . ." And, grabbing a soda siphon from the bar, she drenched Signora Strega-Borgia in its contents.

Once again, the cocktail lounge fell silent.

"Dear me," said Signora Strega-Borgia in arctic tones. "I

think you can stop *squirting,* Mrs. Fforbes-Campbell. The dress is ruined. Antique velvet doesn't put up with such clumsy treatment—but you couldn't be expected to know that, could you? It belonged to my grandmother, designed especially for her by Schiaparelli herself. Still . . . ," she said, brightening considerably and drawing her husband close, ". . . the replacement cost should more than cover our hotel bill for the next few weeks."

She turned back to Morty, who stood gasping behind the bar, his mouth opening and closing like a stranded cod. "I think we'll pass on your *interesting* little wine, Mr. Fforbes-Campbell. Instead, let's have a glass of your finest champagne for everyone in the lounge and a bucket with four straws for my dear beasts and Tock."

Morty was stunned. Finest champagne? Twenty or so bottles at one hundred and seventy-two pounds each? He rubbed his hands in glee.

"*And,* Mrs. Fforbes-Campbell," added Signora Strega-Borgia, "*that* will be on the house. Against the damage to my dress, you understand."

At a table by the window, the group of American lawyers on vacation stood up and cheered. The prospect of *Mermaid v. Morty* more than made up for their lack of Nessie sightings.

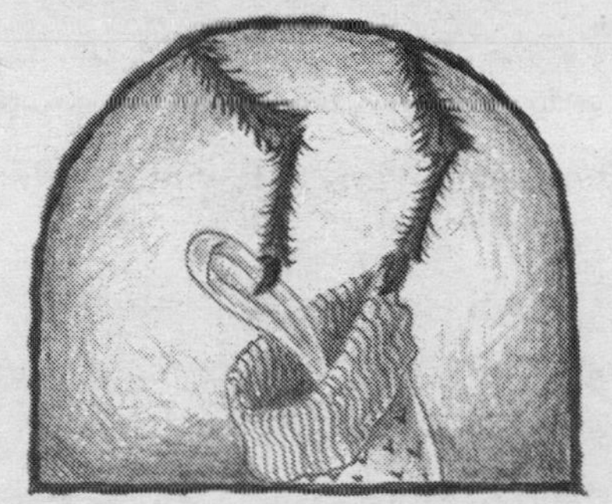

Dodgy Santa

Huddled in a forgotten corner of the attic at StregaSchloss, Tarantella shivered. "How *could* she? How COULD she?" she demanded, addressing the rafters. "Thoughtlessly, heartlessly abandoned. Forgotten. Overlooked. After all I've done for her, and her miserable family—the ungrateful bizzem of a biped." Tarantella paused to stuff another desiccated fly into her underfilled Christmas stocking. "Where's my Christmas present? Where's my annual reward for being such a perfect pet? Where's Pandora?" The spider pouted in a fashion that would have given any self-respecting bluebottle nightmares, then added a deceased daddy longlegs to the stocking. "Not seen hide nor hair of her for three weeks. Not even a postcard. Faithless Pandora. Leaving me with uncultured heathens like rats for company. . . ."

The distant clatter of a diesel engine broke into Tarantella's thoughts and she paused, arrested in mid-rant. Closer now it came, negotiating the moat and pulling up in front of the deserted StregaSchloss. Tarantella instantly relented. "I take it all back. Better late than never. . . . I wonder what she's brought for me?"

Far below, van doors opened and slammed. Tarantella scampered to the cobwebby attic window and peered out through the snowflakes. "Dubious company she's keeping," she observed, noting the four stocky men unloading ladders and ropes from the back of their van. Incorrectly assuming that Pandora was already inside the house, Tarantella leapt across the attic to stand in wait by the trapdoor. "Come on, come *on*," she muttered impatiently.

Clanking and banging came from the scaffold wrapped round the outside of StregaSchloss, and muffled thuds and gruff voices filtered up from the hallway. "This way," came a shout, followed by the sound of boots clattering on the stone stairs.

"It's a right pain in the backside, this. Christmas Eve, and here we are, working. What's the boss up to?"

"Don't know, mate. Just get the roof off, lose the slates in the loch, and no questions asked."

Tarantella puzzled over this. *Get the roof off?* What was going on? The attic was quite cold enough, thank you, without taking the roof off. And *lose the slates in the loch?* That sounded a mite extravagant. . . . The spider crept behind an old cabin trunk and waited.

Seconds later, the trapdoor creaked open, and a silhouetted figure swept a flashlight round the attic. "Pass me your crowbar, Malky," it said, hauling itself inelegantly into the attic, "and the wrecking bar and angle grinder."

Thumps and crashes came from the roof above. Something's gone horribly wrong, Tarantella decided. This is definitely *not* Santa Claus on my roof, and by the sound of things, this isn't going to *be* my roof for much longer. . . . A distant series of shattering crashes confirmed her assumptions. Through the attic window, it appeared to be snowing slates. Hundreds of them, flying through the air and landing with a crash on the flagstones below. An arctic wind blew through centuries of cobwebs strung across the eaves, and snowflakes began to dust the attic floor. The wind picked Tarantella up and blew her across the floorboards. Oh, my word, she thought, woman the lifeboats, mayday, mayday, help, police. Then she looked up. She could see the night sky through the rafters now. It looked black and bleak and cheerless. Straddled across the pockmarked timbers, a man levered off slates with a crowbar and hurled them into space.

Tarantella ran across the attic floor and skidded to a stop at a disused chimney stack that ran the full height of StregaSchloss, from the attic down to the kitchen. Peering through a hole in the chimney breast, she tutted mildly. "Dear, dear. Lift's out of action. *Such* a nuisance. I suppose that means I'll have to use the stairs."

With a backward glance at the rapidly vanishing roof, and using a flurry of snowflakes to camouflage her hasty exit, Tarantella headed for the trapdoor.

Getting Stuffed

Christmas Day dawned wet and sleety. Sensing that this day was extra special, Damp roused her parents from their champagne-drenched slumbers at five-thirty a.m. She dealt with the contents of her stocking in two seconds flat, and happily spent the next two hours trying to poke melting chocolate coins between the clamped lips of her parents.

In their shared room, Pandora and Mrs. McLachlan woke at a more civilized hour, bid each other a sleepy good morning, and rolled over to go back to sleep again. On the foot of their beds, lumpy stockings lay unopened.

Woken by Latch's extended sneezing and nose-blowing session, Titus pried his eyes open. Christmas! he thought, and then, remembering that he was too cool for such things, thought, Oh, yeah, Christmas. There was a large red stocking at the foot of his bed! Oh, yeah, the stocking. Titus scratched an armpit in a thoughtful fashion and tried to yawn insouciantly.

Two seconds later, unable to restrain himself any longer, he somersaulted to the end of the bed, grabbed his stocking, and tipped it upside down on the floor.

Titus was simultaneously cramming chocolate reindeer down his throat and loading a brand-new copy of *Schlock-Horror IV* onto his laptop when Latch emerged sniffing from the bathroom, clutching a box of tissues since his seasonal cold was currently at its peak in terms of mucus production. Titus blinked. Latch was wearing a lounge suit that looked as if it had been salvaged from the wreck of the *Titanic*. Furthermore, he'd cut himself shaving, and a thin trail of blood was trickling down his chin. Briefly, the thought occurred to Titus that he could offer to dab Latch's chin, thus gaining a drop of the butler's blood for cloning purposes, but remembering his success of the night before, he decided that enough was enough. He wondered if Pandora had forgiven him yet. . . .

He didn't have to wonder for too long. Meeting his sibling on the way down to breakfast, he noticed that her left thumb was heavily bandaged.

"Aaargh! It's Psycho-Titus! Keep him *away* from me," Pandora said, clutching Mrs. McLachlan for protection.

"What's she on about?" Titus attempted injured innocence.

"Last night, Titus. Remember? My poor thumb?" Pandora turned to explain to Mrs. McLachlan. "He appeared in my room, black cloak, fangs, full-on vampire, and sank his teeth into my hand. . . ."

"Pardon?" Titus looked blank. "I did *what*?"

"You bit me," said Pandora. "Hard. You drew blood. So I had to hit you with the first thing that came to hand."

"Which was?" Mrs. McLachlan frowned.

"What are you on about?" Titus interrupted. "I was in bed. All night. Asleep, not prowling round the hotel. You're blathering, Pan. Or dreaming. Either way, I think you need therapy."

"So what's this, then?" Pandora waved her thumb in Titus's face. "Or that?" She grabbed her brother's hair, pulling back his bangs to expose a lump the size of a small egg. "Here, look. I did that. With my shoe."

"I wondered where that lump came from. . . ." Titus absentmindedly rubbed his head, then looked up at his sister, as if the thought had just occurred to him. "Oh, heck—d'you think I bit you when I was sleepwalking?"

"That's quite *enough,*" interrupted Mrs. McLachlan in tones that brooked no dissent. "I'm ashamed of the pair of you. Biting and hitting. Any more of this nonsense and you can both go in the stable block with the beasts. Now. Not another word. Let us all go downstairs and have breakfast like civilized human beings, not little heathens."

Over the muted strains of Christmas carols, the Strega-Borgia clan assembled in the dining room could hear the unmistakable din of crashing cutlery and clattering saucepans. Mrs. Fforbes-Campbell was not in a festive mood. The previous evening's wine tasting had left a bitter taste in her mouth, coupled with a thumping headache and an overweening desire to have her revenge on Signora Strega-Borgia. To make matters worse, in her three a.m. search for her infallible headache remedy, Mrs. Fforbes-Campbell had discovered that her crocodile-skin handbag had gone missing. Her temper, usually maintained at a temperature just below simmering point, boiled over.

"You must have seen it, you useless MORON!" she yelled at her husband. "I had it yesterday, in the kitchen. If you hadn't pickled what few remaining brain cells you possessed, you'd be able to remember where I left it. . . ."

Mortimer groaned. Seeking to deflect attention from himself, he picked on the most likely suspect. "Probably been nicked, old girl. Wouldn't put it past that ghastly Borgia chappie, what?"

The ghastly Borgia chappie buttered a round of toast and passed it to the equally ghastly Borgia crocodile. "Tock," he said, attempting a stern manner, "would you happen to know anything about a missing crocodile-skin handbag?"

Tock's dripping spoonful of prunes halted in midair. The crocodile opened his eyes wide and approximated an expression of puzzled innocence. Beside him, Ffup blushed and Sab busied himself with the contents of the marmalade dish.

"It might improve the atmosphere in the hotel if you were to return it," suggested Signor Strega-Borgia, adding, "Anonymously. That is, if you know where it is."

Tock was about to deny all knowledge of the missing handbag when Mrs. Fforbes-Campbell stalked into the dining room. She looked every bit as ill as she felt.

Pandora's eyes rolled backward in her head as she beheld the proprietrix's ostrich-feather-trimmed cardigan, her leopard-skin leggings, and her calfskin boots. "I've suddenly lost my appetite," she remarked, standing up.

"How *interesting,*" said Mrs. Fforbes-Campbell. "I've suddenly lost my handbag."

Tock slid sideways off his chair and, followed by his fellow beasts, vanished in the direction of the gardens. Pandora and Titus headed upstairs to their bedrooms and Mrs. McLachlan and Latch made themselves scarce. Mrs. Fforbes-Campbell looked round the suddenly deserted dining room. "Was it something I said?" she asked, slipping into the empty chair beside Signora Strega-Borgia. "Are you going to join us for lunch today? Very traditional fare, I'm afraid. Roast goose and all the trimmings. Plum pudding—all those ghastly calories. . . . Luciano, you simply must have some of my special stuffing—it's absolutely *heavenly*. Not for us, dear," she said, patting Signora Strega-Borgia conspiratorially on the arm. "Not if we need to watch our figures . . ."

Signora Strega-Borgia poured herself another cup of coffee, ostentatiously ladled four spoonfuls of sugar and a generous dollop of cream into it, and swallowed the lot in one elegant gulp. "I'd love to try your stuffing, *dear,*" she said sweetly, "since I don't have to watch my figure—I let Luciano do that for me."

Comparisons are odious, but if asked to name her favorite present of that strange Christmas, Pandora would have nominated the tiny pot of cream given to her by Mrs. McLachlan. Compared to that tiny bejeweled tub of vanishing cream, all CDs, clothes, toys, and books paled into insignificance. Even Titus conceded that vanishing cream was seriously cool after Pandora had demonstrated its miraculous powers during a Brussels sprout episode at lunchtime.

"Just eat them, darling," advised Signora Strega-Borgia, "and then we'll have pudding."

"Frankly, I'd rather die," muttered Titus, glaring at the little mushy green cannonballs clustered round the rim of his plate.

"TITUS!"

Titus looked up from his plate. His father was glaring at him, but given that Signor Strega-Borgia had held his face muscles in the Grimace Position throughout the starter (prawns Marie-Rose), the soup (broccoli and Stilton), and the sorbet (avocado and lime), the effect of his glare was somewhat diluted.

"Titus," Pandora hissed, "cause a distraction and I'll make your sprouts disappear."

Titus didn't need to be asked twice. He reached out for the gravy boat and skillfully toppled a teetering arrangement of fir cones and fruit that the management had provided to grace each table in the dining room. "Ooops. Sorry," Titus mumbled, joining in the under-the-table scrum to catch tumbling apples, pomegranates, and fir cones that cascaded from their table. When the family reseated themselves to continue their meal, Titus saw that Pandora had been as good as her word. "*Wicked,*" he whispered, attacking the rest of his meal with renewed relish.

Much later, bloated and bilious, all the guests and staff collapsed on sofas in the residents' lounge to attempt to cram in mince pies and postprandial drinks before their stomachs finally exploded. Titus took this opportunity to disappear in search of an incubator. Since the previous evening he'd been in possession of the blood, the infrared facility, and, in a moment of inspiration, had realized that his mother's Knot-regurgitated ectoplasm would provide the perfect growth medium for his diy-clones. All he needed now was an incubator. . . .

He had a pretty good idea where to find one. Over lunch, he'd overheard a most promising conversation between Latch and Mrs. McLachlan, who, along with the rest of the family, had avoided the roast goose completely.

"I don't think that has been properly cooked," Mrs. McLachlan said under her breath as she passed the platter to Latch without taking any for herself. Latch observed the pink slabs of meat studded with congealed goose fat and, with a shudder, passed the plate onward to Tock.

"I'll pass," the crocodile decided. "Raw goose for you, Ffup?"

"It's a breeding ground for all sorts of bacteria," Mrs. McLachlan advised, passing a tureen of roast potatoes on to Latch.

"Heavens knows what horrors are growing in it," agreed the butler, spooning a consolatory half-dozen potatoes onto his plate.

With this in mind, Titus headed for the kitchen and, some minutes later, crept across the reception area on his way upstairs, carrying a large china platter on which lay the carcass of the goose. He discovered that it was still warm when he stuffed the cavity beneath the bird's rib cage with ectoplasm. Being ectoplasm, it slithered and flopped, disobeying the rules of gravity, oozing from between the ribs, with some of it vaporizing in a misty swirl over the china platter.

Titus had to admit that this was one of the most unpleasant tasks he'd ever undertaken in the name of scientific discovery. It was about to get worse. Pushing the handkerchief stained with Pandora's blood into the congealing warmth of the ectoplasm-stuffed goose made his stomach lurch sickeningly into his throat. And when Titus stabbed himself in the finger with his mother's brooch pin and caught sight of his own blood, he had to lie down immediately. Overhead, the room spun slowly round and, just to put the lid on his discomfort, the smell of clotting goose fat clung to his hair, his clothes, his—Titus bolted for the bathroom and was noisily and copiously sick.

Ten minutes later, pale and wobbly, he was ready to achieve his goal. The goose was balanced on top of the radiator to keep it warm. His laptop hummed quietly, its infrared port pointed directly at the goose's vent, and the bloodstained ectoplasm bubbled and heaved nicely within. On the laptop screen, a menu appeared:

Clone monitor

Units?	Male [4]	Female [2]		
Size?	100% ☒	Other ☐		
Quality?	Best ☒	Normal ☐	Draft ☐	
Color?	Black ☐	White ☒	Brown ☐	Gold ☐
	Other ☐	(e.g., Pink, Olive, Cream, etc.)		
Action?	Enter ☐	Pause ☒	Abort ☐	

"Yessss!" Titus hissed. "Yes, yes, yes, YES!"

"I thought I heard you in here," said a voice. "Phwoaaarr—what's that sme—? TITUS? What on earth are you doing with that *goose*?"

Titus turned. Pandora stood in the open doorway, her face pale, her eyes saucerlike in total incomprehension. Unnoticed, Damp wobbled across the carpet toward the radiator. She, too, was somewhat puzzled by the reappearance of the lunchtime goose, but she put that mystery to one side when she caught sight of Titus's laptop. It glowed invitingly, cursor a-blink, the background music of the diy-clones program drawing Damp in closer.

"I'm . . . um . . . um," Titus mumbled, horribly aware that his stomach, which he fervently hoped might have calmed down, hadn't.

"That is *so* disgusting, Titus. Eurrgh. Gross. Can't you open a window? It *honks* in here—bleurch, you're *sick,* Titus."

"Mmrghh . . . ," Titus agreed.

Damp pressed a key on the piano thing, but to her disappointment, absolutely nothing happened. She peered at the screen, patted the keyboard with an open hand, paused, and then thumped several keys simultaneously. In the background, Pandora struggled with the window fastening, but being a hotel window, it steadfastly refused to open. Damp gave a small squawk and fell backward onto her bottom. The screen turned bright blood-red, and the programmed music was abruptly replaced with a deep and irrevocable hum.

"OH MY GLAARGHHH!" Titus, torn between rescuing his cloning project and the overwhelming desire to void his stomach of all its contents, achieved the best of both worlds. He threw up over his laptop, but not before he caught the ominous message written on its screen:

Cloning activated successfully

It wasn't until several hours later, after much mopping and scraping and many recriminations and apologies, that Titus and Pandora were sufficiently reconciled to discover deep in the clone monitor menu that Damp had inadvertently altered

Titus's game plan somewhat. Brother clutched sister in utter horror as both read onscreen:

Size	**10%**
Quality	**Draft**
Color	**Pink**

and, more importantly,

Units (total) **500**

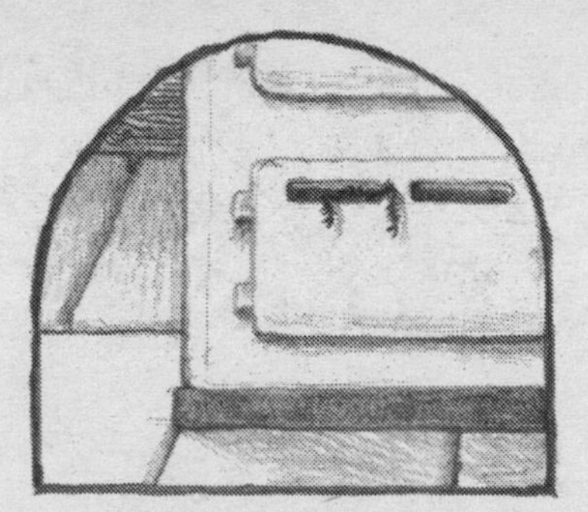

Dirty Deeds

In the kitchen at StregaSchloss, Tarantella was freezing cold. Outside the kitchen windows, the snow had turned overnight to sleety rain interspersed with dazzling winter sunshine, but the interior of the house bore more resemblance to an overenthusiastic freezer than a dwelling. To add to the general misery, the blizzard that had fallen through the detiled roof had thawed, soaked through the entire house, and begun to drip into the kitchen. Tarantella took shelter in the plate-warming oven of the range, which, though cold, was at least dry. She had been spinning a lair of spider silk when she heard noises from outside.

Tip-tap, tip-tap came a faint percussive footfall along the kitchen corridor. Peering through the air vents in the oven, Tarantella could just see a furry apparition picking its way delicately across the flooded kitchen floor.

"Hugh-hoo?" caroled a female voice. "Darling? Where are you?"

From the kitchen garden, a measured tread could be heard. The garden door opened and, preceded by a cloud of smoke, a man stepped into the kitchen. "Ffion, you made it," he said.

To Tarantella's disgust, the female furry thing scampered across the floor and glued its mouthparts to those of the smoky man. Both participants in this ghastly biped ritual squirmed and groaned, finally breaking apart and gazing hungrily at each other. "Get on with it," muttered Tarantella. "Just gobble him up, there's a good girl."

"Hugh, darling, I can't tell you how I've missed you," the furry one said. "And on Christmas Eve, having to pretend that you were just a friend. . . ."

"Agony, my sweet," the smoky man agreed, "but not for too much longer now. . . ."

The couple gazed around. From the kitchen ceiling, a steady dripping indicated that StregaSchloss was in dire need of repair.

The smoky man gave a little grunt of satisfaction. "The boys did well last night," he said. "That roof's totally ruined now. When the Sega-Porsches find out that the repair bill is now in the millions, they'll be only too glad to sell up and go."

"What a dump," said the furry one, splashing across the floor. "I *knew* she was a slob, despite all her airs and graces. What a *pigsty*. D'you know, Hugh, I could swear I just saw something move in that corner over there."

"Probably a rat," said the smoky man. "I wouldn't worry about it. When we raze this monstrosity to the ground, the rats will be destroyed with it."

From her quarters in the pantry, Multitudina gave a squeak of outrage.

"Eughh," said the furry biped, "I *heard* it. We used to have them running around at the Auchenlochtermuchty Arms, but I soon got rid of them. With the same rat poison I've been sprinkling in Morty's nightcap, actually. . . ."

The smoky man shuddered and drew deeply on his cigar. "What a ruthless pair we make," he observed. "One intent on eliminating her husband, the other determined to demolish this crumbling heap, closely followed by his business partner. . . ."

"Perfectly matched, darling," the furry one breathed. "Nothing can hope to stand in our way. Nothing will be allowed to."

"And when your husband finally succumbs to your deadly attentions, and I despatch that moronic but useful Vincent Bella-Vista. . . ."

"Don't forget his *frightful* girlfriend, darling. We don't want her blowing the whistle on our little enterprise, do we?"

"Who could ever forget Vadette?" the smoky man said. "However, I predict with absolute certainty that Vadette will take her own life in an excess of grief over losing Vinnie. Then we flog Morty's hotel, flog this crumbling heap and its extensive grounds to the Nuclear Waste Reprocessing Conglomerate, and head for the sun. Together—at last."

"Oh, Hugh, darling, you're a genius." Once more, the furry one advanced on the smoky man and glued her mouthparts to his.

"Dis*gus*ting," remarked Tarantella with relish, settling comfortably in front of the oven vents, all the beter to spy on the proceedings. She nibbled at a mummified wasp that had blundered fatally into the plate-warming oven the previous summer. "Devious, delinquent, and demonic, in fact. Downright dastardly—but *utterly* fascinating, nonetheless." She leapt up to the vent and gazed out into the kitchen. To her disappointment, fur and smoke had gone. Scanning the whole kitchen, Tarantella spotted movement under the table. Since it appeared that the coast was clear, she squeezed through the air vent to investigate.

What she discovered swimming in a pool of snowmelt under the kitchen table caused her to bolt at top speed back to the safety of the oven. "Oh, my word!" she gasped. "Something truly weird is happening. A microscopic throng of shrunken squaddies appears to be materializing out there. . . ."

Bracing herself for another look, Tarantella peered through the gap. Hundreds of tiny somethings were wading across a pool of water underneath the kitchen table, heading for dry land. Tiny somethings clad in skirts waving pointy sticks in a decidedly unfriendly manner. Tiny somethings that appeared to be growing by the minute. Tarantella blinked. The low-slanting winter sunshine reflected off hundreds of tiny shields advancing out from under the table. The forgotten tincture of Ffuptooth had mixed with the snowmelt dripping through the kitchen ceiling, and from this combination, a battalion of tiny warriors had sprung.

Retreating to the back of the plate-warming oven, Tarantella knelt down on all eight of her hairy knees. "Pandora," she beseeched. "PANDORA—*please* come home."

Making a Killing

Boxing Day at StregaSchloss had traditionally been spent in a heap of half-built Lego models, picking at the cold remains of Christmas lunch, and later, in the company of mountains of tangerines and boxes of chocolates, watching classic films in a room that always smelt of wood smoke and pine needles. The Strega-Borgias always took the phone off the hook, the great-great-great-great-great-great-grandmother out of the freezer, and finished the day by playing charades in the library. Not so this year. On this Boxing Day, the Auchenlochtermuchty Arms offered little in the way of seasonal comfort. It appeared to be a day in the hotel management calendar for which the word "anticlimax" had been invented.

Aware that her siblings were not best pleased with her after the catastrophic interference with Titus's laptop, Damp grizzled and clung limpet-like to Mrs. McLachlan. Titus and Pandora were conspicuous by their absence, and sneezing explosively,

Latch had gone out for a lochside trek with the beasts, and, to their dismay, Signor and Signora Strega-Borgia found that they had company in the residents' lounge. Sprawled across the only comfortable sofa were Vinnie and Vadette, wreathed in a cloud of cigarette smoke. Since the only alternative to sharing the lounge with this pair was to return to their bedroom, Signor and Signora Strega-Borgia sighed in stereo and joined the builder and his girlfriend.

Signora Strega-Borgia folded her legs into a rigid settle while her husband paced moodily in front of the bookshelves by the fire. "Baci," he said, "can I get you something to read?"

"Why not?" said Signora Strega-Borgia. "Pass me that book on financial management for the homeless businesswoman, would you?"

"You don't want to read that stuff in a book," said Vincent Bella-Vista, coughing wetly as he threw his cigarette in the vague direction of the fireplace. "No one ever learnt anything from *books*. They're total rubbish."

"Really?" said Signora Strega-Borgia, catching her husband's eye as they raised eyebrows in tandem. "You've read them all, have you?"

"Waste of time, the lot of 'em. . . ." The builder waved dismissively at the bookcase.

"Especially the ones with pictures on the cover," added Vadette, not to be outdone. "Why, anyone would think that only floozies and con men came to the Auchenlochtermuchty Arms. . . ."

"Don't they?" murmured Signora Strega-Borgia, taking in Vinnie's natty brown pinstripe suit and Vadette's pink lurex mini-skirt that barely covered her stomach, let alone her vast thighs.

"Nah. . . ." Vinnie held out an open packet of cigarettes, unaware of the veiled insult. "This place, now, this is what I call *class*. Cut above the rest—know what I mean?"

"No," said Signora Strega-Borgia in answer to both the offer of a cigarette and Vinnie's question, "I don't, actually."

"Ages the skin dreadfully," came a voice from the doorway. "Makes one smell like an old ashtray, doesn't it, Vadette, pet?"

Vadette inhaled deeply and glowered up at Mrs. Fforbes-Campbell. "I'd rather smell like an ashtray than a butcher's shop—Fifi, what the hell is that you're wearing?"

"This old thing?" Mrs. Fforbes-Campbell laughed girlishly. "Oh, it's my Dior, actually. Baby sealskin with whalebone corsetry—marvelous what you can do with a few bits of dead animal, isn't it?"

Signora Strega-Borgia blanched as the manageress bore down on where she was sitting.

"I'm afraid there's been a complaint," Mrs. Fforbes-Campbell confided. "One of our American guests—lawyer chappie in room forty-three, the tedious type who always threatens to sue if the soup's too soupy or the sheets too . . . Anyway, he rang downstairs to say he's trying to sleep, but the racket coming from your son's room is making it *quite* impossible."

"Titus?" said Signora Strega-Borgia. "I'll go and see."

"And," continued Mrs. Fforbes-Campbell, "while you're up there—heavens, I don't know how to put this without causing offense. . . ." The manageress leaned in close to where Signora Strega-Borgia sat rigid with embarrassment. "The chambermaid has complained about the *smell* in your son's room. Apparently, it's so bad that she's flatly refusing to go in there and clean."

"I'll go immediately." Signora Strega-Borgia unfolded herself from the settle and ran upstairs.

"I do apologize," said Signor Strega-Borgia. "I'm sure my wife will sort it out."

"Luciano," said Mrs. Fforbes-Campbell, turning on him a smile of dazzling whiteness, "let me introduce you to one of my dearest friends, Vincent Bella-Vista."

"Luciano Strega-Borgia," said Signor Strega-Borgia, reaching over to shake the builder's outstretched hand, "from StregaSchloss, just outside the village. Do you live locally?"

Feeling distinctly overlooked, Vadette thrust out her hand. "We live in the bungalow on the hill where the old public toilets used to be. Vinnie built it last year and we just added on a sauna and a big garage for our matching white vans. I'm Vadette, affianced to dear Vincent here. I help him with his business."

At sea in Vadette's tide of domestic information, Signor Strega-Borgia turned back to the builder and attempted to appear interested. "Do you work locally, Mr. Bella-Vista? Living out at StregaSchloss, we're a bit out of touch with what goes on in the village. . . ."

Vincent Bella-Vista lit a fresh cigarette and smiled up at Signor Strega-Borgia. "I do a bit of this and a bit of that," he confessed modestly. "Demolition and re-building, if you know what I mean."

"All too well," said Signor Strega-Borgia. "My family and I

have had to decamp here temporarily because of a problem with our roof."

Vincent Bella-Vista sighed sympathetically. "Those old properties—waste of money, if you ask me—cost a fortune to repair. There comes a time when it's far simpler just to knock the whole thing down and start again. . . . StregaSchloss, did you say? Down on the sea loch? Must be—what, six, seven hundred years old?"

"Give or take the odd century," agreed Signor Strega-Borgia. "Been in the family since the year dot."

"Roof's going to set you back a bit, mate." The builder grinned. "Ever thought about selling up and going for something a bit more manageable?"

"Frequently," muttered Signor Strega-Borgia, cast into immediate gloom by the reminder of what the roof repair was going to cost.

"I could do you a deal, squire." Vincent Bella-Vista winked at Mrs. Fforbes-Campbell, who was paying close attention to this conversation. "Take the old place off your hands, do you a nice five-bedroomed special over the other side of the village on the Bogginview estate . . . ?"

"Um . . . ," said Signor Strega-Borgia, floundering in a vision of life without StregaSchloss. "But we keep beasts . . . staff . . . a cryogenically preserved great-great-great-great-great-great-grandmother."

"No problemski—we could throw in a garden shed and a double garage as well." Sensing that his potential client was beginning to panic, the builder backed off. "Tell you what—you go away and have a think about it. Talk it over with your wife.

See what the kiddies think. . . . Here's my card—I'd be happy to talk you through it anytime you want."

"Vinnie, you're such a relentless businessman," Mrs. Fforbes-Campbell cooed, gliding over and wrapping a protective arm round Signor Strega-Borgia. "Leave this poor man alone. It's a holiday today, remember? Now, can I get anyone a drink? Luciano? What'll you have?"

Outside, a crunching of gravel alerted the occupants of the residents' lounge to the arrival of a police car.

"Oh, Lord," muttered Mrs. Fforbes-Campbell, "what do *they* want? I'll just go and see—back in a tick. . . ."

In the bedroom that Titus shared with Latch and five hundred pink clones, the arrival of their mother threw Titus and Pandora into a panic. Titus grabbed the foul goose carcass from its hiding place in the wardrobe, leapt into the bathroom, and locked himself in. Pandora opened the door to admit her mother.

"Euchhh—what a *frightful* smell." Signora Strega-Borgia gagged as a wave of decomposing goose rolled greasily into the corridor. "What *is* going on?"

"Titus . . . um . . . it's the goose," Pandora improvised wildly. "He's got diarrhea—Titus, not the goose. It's really awful—he's been in there for *ages*."

Signora Strega-Borgia edged into the bedroom holding a handkerchief to her mouth. "Poor Titus," she said, calling through the bathroom door. "Darling? Can I get you anything? Some ice water?"

From the bathroom came a yell and an accompanying crash of china. "Oh, no—the goose! Aaaargh! Oh, yeurchhh! *Stop* it!"

"What is he saying?" Signora Strega-Borgia pressed her ear up to the bathroom door. "Who is he talking to? Stop *what*? What is he doing in there?"

"It's . . . um . . . very violent." Pandora grabbed her mother's arm. "The diarrhea, I mean. Don't worry, I think he's nearly over the worst of it."

"Not down the *toilet*," wailed Titus. "*Behave*, would you? Stand *still*. And don't *hiss*."

"Hiss?" said Signora Strega-Borgia. "What . . . ?"

"It's the gas," explained Pandora, steering her mother toward the door to the corridor. "He's awfully flatulent, poor Titus. And he's probably hallucinating. . . . Could you find him some more toilet paper? And a cup of tea? I'll go and try to get him into bed." At last Pandora succeeded in pushing her mother back out into the corridor. Locking the door behind her, she headed to the bathroom. "Let me in," she demanded. "Mum's gone to get you some tea and toilet paper."

The bathroom door opened a crack, allowing Pandora to squeeze inside. Titus was pink with effort, but not half as pink as the tiny clones that were grouped in a hissing huddle in the shower. The bathroom floor was littered with shards of shattered platter and the walls were awash with grease from the exploded goose. The stench was overpowering. Titus looked up at his sister. His face was streaked with tears, rancid gooseflesh dangled from his hair, and he looked utterly defeated.

"Oh, my God, Pandora," he whispered. "What have I *done*?"

Bad News All Round

Bearing a tray with glasses, two rolls of toilet paper, a pot of tea, and a bottle of whisky, Mrs. Fforbes-Campbell led the policemen into the residents' lounge. The Strega-Borgias were attempting to discuss the workings of their son's gastrointestinal tract with Mrs. McLachlan, and Damp was sitting on a sofa playing with her favorite Christmas present, a teddy that displayed alarmingly dysfunctional lip synch.

"Thank you," said Mrs. McLachlan, plucking the tray from the manageress's hands. "We'll take these up to Titus, the poor lamb. I'm quite sure it was that undercooked goose that's to blame." She removed the whisky bottle and the glasses and glared at Mrs. Fforbes-Campbell. "Not content with poisoning his poor tummy with your cooking, are you trying to destroy his wee liver with alcohol?" And with a loud disapproving snort, she slammed the whisky and glasses down on a tabletop and strode off upstairs.

Mrs. Fforbes-Campbell blinked rapidly then, recovering her poise, oiled across the room to where Signor Strega-Borgia stood by the fireside. "Luciano, pet," she soothed, holding out a brimming glass, "I think you might be needing this. It's bad news, I'm afraid. . . . I'll let the police constable fill you in on the details."

One of the two policemen stepped forward. "Sir," he began, flicking through a small black notebook, "are you Luciano Strega-Borgia, resident and owner of the property known as StregaSchloss, situated on the west shore of Lochnagargoyle?"

Signor Strega-Borgia sat down abruptly on an oversprung armchair. The resultant bounce caused the whisky in his glass to slop out over his knees. "I am," he confirmed. "Wha . . . ?"

"It's about your house, sir." The constable dropped his eyes to his notebook, unsure of how to continue. "Well . . . urr . . . to cut a long story short, it's wrecked."

"WHAAT?" Signor Strega-Borgia bounced back out of his seat.

"Darling." Signora Strega-Borgia took his arm. "Calm yourself. . . ."

"It's the roof, sir," the policeman continued. "Must have blown off in the night. A patrol car was passing around dawn this morning. Seven-fifty a.m., to be precise. Our officers Macbeth and McDuff noticed that the silhouette of your property appeared to have altered considerably. Upon closer examination, they discovered that the roof timbers were exposed, the slates had vanished, and a quantity of snow had fallen into your attic. We've taken the precaution of placing warning signs outside to this effect, and cordoned off the whole area in the interests of public safety. . . ."

"But, but . . ." Signor Strega-Borgia groped for understanding and failed utterly. "That's IMPOSSIBLE!" he shrieked.

"Darling, calm down. . . ."

"Roofs don't just *vanish*!"

"This one did," the other policeman muttered.

"But the slates. Where? Surely they must be . . . ?"

"My colleagues did wonder about that, sir, but there was no sign of them—no broken slates in the courtyard, nothing at all."

Delighted that his business partner had succeeded in destroying the roof at StregaSchloss, Vincent Bella-Vista coughed from a corner of the lounge where he and Vadette had been avidly eavesdropping. "Must've been the wind," he remarked, adding, "Cost a fortune to replace them. Hundreds of thousands. Millions. . . ."

Signor Strega-Borgia paled. "We don't *have* millions. Oh, the poor house. After all these years, all those generations of our family living and dying at StregaSchloss. . . ."

"Can we go and salvage some of our possessions?" Signora Strega-Borgia said. "The books? The furniture? Oh, Luciano, whatever are we going to do?"

"I wouldn't advise it today, madam." The policeman replaced his notebook in his breast pocket, and frowned. "The property is in a parlous state. Dangerous, in fact—there's a possibility that the upper floors might collapse. . . . You'll probably have to put scaffolding across the main timbers to stop the whole thing folding up like a pack of cards."

"We'll get the experts in once the holidays are over," the other policeman added. "See what, if anything, they can do to save it. But the worst-case scenario is that they have to place a compulsory demolition order on it, and unfortunately, you'd have to pay for that."

"Cost a king's ransom," another voice added cheerfully from the door of the lounge. "Allow me to introduce myself, officer. Name's Pylum-Haight. Hugh Pylum-Haight. My firm was just about to undertake repairs to the roof at StregaSchloss. Could I be of some assistance?"

"Is that your black BMW in the car park, sir?" one of the policemen asked irrelevantly, looking out the window. "The one with pink dots all over the hood? And its lights left on?"

"Pink dots? I *don't* think so. Mine's black all over." Hugh Pylum-Haight crossed the lounge and peered out at the parking lot. "What on earth are those? Excuse me just one moment. . . ."

While the puzzled car owner stepped outside, Vincent Bella-Vista swooped down on the stunned Strega-Borgias. "Bad luck, that," he said, patting Signor Strega-Borgia chummily on the arm. "The offer still stands, you know. Always glad to help someone out when fate deals them a curve ball. Just give me a bell when you're ready." Clasping Vadette's arm, he steered her rapidly out of the lounge, followed by Mrs. Fforbes-Campbell.

"Will that be all, officer?" Signora Strega-Borgia attempted a wan smile. "My husband and I will need some time to decide what to do. . . ."

"We'll be in touch when we've had a word with the experts, madam," said the policeman. "Let you know what they decide."

Both policemen turned and left the Strega-Borgias to their misery. Signor Strega-Borgia took his wife's hands in his. "We're ruined, Baci," he said bleakly. "We're going to have to leave StregaSchloss. The children are going to be devastated. . . ."

"Oh, my poor house," Signora Strega-Borgia burst into tears. "Our lovely home. We should never have left."

From the parking lot, muffled curses drifted into the residents' lounge. Hugh Pylum-Haight was attempting to remove the splattered remains of several suicidal clones from the hood of his beloved BMW. Since the clones had launched themselves onto his car from several floors up, their flattened bodies bore more resemblance to pink blancmange than to homunculi, but unlike blancmange, they were proving impossible to remove. Unaware that he had an audience, Hugh Pylum-Haight let loose a stream of toe-curling invective as he dabbed ineffectually on the car hood with a tissue.

Behind him, Tock rooted in a recently exhumed crocodile-skin handbag and produced a packet of scented wipes. "Try one of these," the crocodile offered, extending a helpful claw.

"Better see if you can burn it off—cleaner that way," Ffup decided. "Stand well back. . . ."

Hugh Pylum-Haight turned round. His audience of watching beasts grinned at him, but the sight of so many teeth bared in greeting failed to give him any comfort whatsoever. "What?" he squeaked, backing away from the beasts' combined grins.

Assuming incorrectly that this meant he had permission to proceed, the dragon stepped forward, bent over the hood of the BMW, took a deep breath, and blasted a vast gout of flame from both nostrils.

"MY CAR!" screamed Hugh Pylum-Haight. "STOP! NO! HELP! POLICE! NO, NO, DON'T DO THAT!"

In the bathroom, Titus carefully placed the last pink clone to fall asleep onto the floor beside its four hundred and three siblings. It hissed faintly as he tucked it in under two leaves of toilet paper. Despite the horrors that he'd recently experienced, Titus felt quite absurdly pleased with himself. He'd managed to remove all traces of rancid goose fat from the five hundred clones by the simple expedient of upending a bottle of shower gel over them, waiting while they squabbled and fought, and turning the shower on them with sufficient force to pin them against the wall of the shower cubicle.

Regrettably, there had been a few casualties along the way: the three dozen that had scaled the heights of the radiator, crawled onto the window ledge, and launched themselves into free fall onto the black car in the parking lot; the many handfuls that Damp had flushed down the toilet; and the one . . .

"Ugh." Titus shivered, his eyes drawn to a tiny pink stain on the carpet, near the door. He could still remember the underfoot hiss, then a pop followed by spreading wetness. . . .

Pandora stuck her head round the bathroom door. The combined snores of the surviving clones had an oddly soothing effect, not unlike the broody cluckings from a crowded henhouse.

"They're really quite sweet," whispered Titus.

"Only when they're asleep. Euchhh, what an effort! I'm never going to have any babies ever ever ever." Pandora pulled her brother out of the bathroom and closed the door behind him. "Right," she said, "we have to do some research. The question is, how big will they grow, and how soon?"

"That's two questions," muttered Titus.

"Whatever." Pandora pointed to the de-goosed laptop. "Come on. You got us into this mess, now get us out of it."

Titus obediently logged on to WWW.DIY-CLONES.COM and began to type out an e-mail, hindered only slightly by Pandora breathing heavily as she read over his shoulder.

helpdesk@diy-clones.com
Dear Helpdesk

"That's not a proper name," complained Pandora. "Honestly, Titus—dumb or what?"

Titus rolled his eyes and re-typed:

Dear Dumborwhat
We've followed yr. instructions and have grown c. 500 clones at 10%, draft (pink). They're quite big now and are very hard to dissipline

"I don't think that's how you—"

"Shut up, Pan. Do you want me to write this or not?" Titus typed on, doggedly paying no heed to the loud sighs coming from his sister.

. . . and we're wondering just how big are they going to get, and when will they finally stop (i.e. be adults)?
Yours sincerely
Titus A. Strega-Borgia (Mr.)

"Is that *it*?" said Pandora. "What about: how do we get rid of them? Can we send them back? Or are we stuck with them for ever and ever?"

“I’ll add on a bit at the end.” Titus’s fingers flew over the keys for a few minutes, then he exhaled noisily, slumped back in his seat, and waited for Pandora to approve his amendments before he pressed ENTER and sent the e-mail. Pandora peered at the screen. Titus had added:

> P.S. We’d be happy to send them back if you would send us your snail-mail address. Or if you would send us some other addresses that might be interested in c. 500 draft, 10% (pink) clones. We’d be very grateful. Or even any suggestions for how my sister and I are supposed to feed c. 500 mouths on our measly pocket-money allowance. Our parents would kill us if they knew. Yours sincerely (again) T. A. S-B.

“Yup. That’s good. I like the last bit,” Pandora approved. “Sort of conveys what deep poo we’re in. Maybe they’ll feel sorry for us. . . .”

Titus pressed ENTER and sat back to wait. His outgoing e-mail crossed with an incoming one and he opened this, noting that it was dated December 25. Reminding himself that it was highly unlikely Santa Claus was on the Net, even if he *did* exist, Titus read on.

“Anything interesting?” yawned Pandora, slumping backward onto Titus’s bed.

“Oh, NO,” Titus groaned. “Listen to this, Pan: ‘Congratulations. Diy-clones are happy to have assisted you with your groundbreaking discovery. We would like to take this opportunity to advise you that your clones, in common with all bio-engineered beings, will experience accelerated aging by a factor of eight thousand six hundred and forty. This means that one minute of real time equals a bioclonic increment of nearly a week.' "

"Urrrgh. What? Why can't they write this sort of stuff in English?" Pandora complained. "What does it all *mean*?"

"*I* don't know." Titus gazed blankly out of the window and frowned. "Out of interest, why are there clouds of black smoke billowing up from the car park?"

"Maybe someone's set their car on fire," said Pandora. "Stop changing the subject. Go on. Read me some more gobbledegook."

Titus continued patiently: " 'One hour of your time is actually one year in clone time, one day for you is almost a staggering quarter century whizzing past on a clone calendar. Therefore, the average life expectancy of your creations is something in the region of three and a half days in your time. . . .' "

"Look," interrupted Pandora, "you've got another e-mail. Surely it's got to be more interesting than this. . . ."

"That'll be them replying." Titus opened the new e-mail on top of the previous one. "Yup. Here we go. . . ."

Brother and sister read in dismay:

Dear T. A. S-B.,
diy-clones@wicked.com is no longer trading and is subject to ongoing investigations by MAFF (the Ministry of Agriculture, Farming, and Fisheries), H&S Exec (the Health and

Safety Executive), OFTEL (the Office of Fair Trading), M&MComm (the Monopolies and Mergers Commission); also the FBI, the CIA, MI5, and Scotland Yard are currently baying for our blood. Our advice would be to log off pronto and forget you ever heard of us. If asked, pretend you found this site by accident. However, we are recommending that all our former clients contact the following sites to assist them with the disposal or otherwise of their unwanted "material."

Sorry, Ms. Dumborwhat

diy-clones@wicked.com

Sites of interest:

libertyclone@siberiansaltmines.com

organic_meat_company.co.uk

pestpatrol.com

wet.affairs@mafia.org.ital

"Help . . . ," said Pandora, unusually at a loss for what to say. "Could we go back to the one before this? The one that I couldn't understand. I think it was saying that they'll only live for a week, at the most. . . ."

Without comment, Titus closed the front e-mail, revealing the previous one underneath. Concentrating mightily to take their minds off the horrors suggested by diy-clones's terminal e-mail, they read:

. . . three and a half days in your time, by which time clones become senile, incontinent,

> and prone to vast mood swings. With this inconvenience in mind, diy-clones would like to recommend the use of readily dissolvable EXIT Powders™ as a quick and painless solution to this problem.

"RIGHT!" bawled Pandora, springing to her feet and crossing to the window. "Let's get some *now*. D'you think we could buy some in Auchenlochtermuchty?"

Titus choked. "But . . . Pandora, that—that's *murder*! We can't do that. They've got as much right to life as we do."

"NO! DON'T SHOOT HIM! THAT'S MURDER! YOU CAN'T DO THAT! HE'S GOT AS MUCH RIGHT TO LIFE AS YOU DO!" Pandora screamed.

"What? What on earth are you on about? Shoot who?" Titus leapt to his feet and crossed to the window where Pandora pointed downward. He leaned out and looked down to the parking lot, where, surrounded by a ring of hysterical guests, enraged management, and terrified beasts, Hugh Pylum-Haight had Ffup pinned to the gravel on the business end of a hunting rifle. Abandoning the slumbering multitudes in the bathroom, Titus and Pandora ran downstairs to rescue their dragon.

"I've got every right to blow your brains out!" the roofer bawled at the dragon. "You've deliberately ruined my car."

"But—but—but I've got rid of the pink blobs for you," Ffup wailed. "I thought you'd be *grateful*, not murderous."

"Hugh . . . HUGH! What on earth are you doing?" Mrs.

Fforbes-Campbell tumbled out of the hotel, closely followed by Mortimer.

"This—this *monster*'s destroyed my car."

"Gosh, I say, old chap, I rather think it has, what?"

"Ffup, come *here,*" commanded Signora Strega-Borgia, appearing at the entrance steps to the hotel, bearing a large leash in her hands.

"I *can't,*" wailed Ffup. "There's a lunatic here with a loaded gun. Help!"

"Oh, for heaven's sake!" Signora Strega-Borgia shouted, finally losing her temper as she pushed her way through the throng in the parking lot. "As if having one's house destroyed overnight isn't enough, now I find a maniac threatening my beloved beast with a deadly weapon. You, sir, are a moron, and this"—she grabbed the rifle and tossed it in a flower bed—"is an obscenity." Seeing the litigious glint in Hugh Pylum-Haight's eyes, she waved him away. "Yes, yes, your *car*. We'll compensate you for the damage—what's a few thousand more when you're facing financial ruin?"

"Actually, Mrs. Sega-Porsche, not a few thousand—forty-eight k plus VAT to be precise." The builder looked round at his audience for support.

"WhatEVER!" bawled Signora Strega-Borgia. "It's only money. Right, my lambs, let's get you out of harm's way in the stable block, shall we?"

The beasts, quite accustomed to being addressed by a collective noun that more accurately described their favorite dinner, lined up obediently by their mistress's side.

"I'll have to ask you to keep those *brutes* under lock and key from now on," said Mrs. Fforbes-Campbell, seizing this opportunity to make her opponent squirm. "They're far too dangerous to be allowed anywhere near the hotel. . . ." She paused, struck by the sight of a familiar object lying abandoned on the gravel of the parking lot. "My bag! What's it doing out here? Eughhh, where on earth has it been?"

On the verge of informing her that he'd once known her handbag to splash in the shallows of the Limpopo River, before it became a handbag, Tock found himself being firmly dragged out of earshot by his beloved mistress. Reading her expression, he gave a little honk of alarm.

"Not one word," said Signora Strega-Borgia, leading the beasts into the chilly gloom of the stable block. "You've done enough damage to last a lifetime, Ffup. And you, Tock, what were you thinking of, burying that handbag then exhuming it again? Don't you think that awful woman will work out that it was you who stole her bag? Yes, yes, I know that it was the decent thing to do, burying your old friend, but he's long dead, well beyond the indignity of being a purse rather than a predator. . . ."

" 'S not fair," Knot complained, throwing himself down on a pile of dank straw. "I didn't do *anything*. . . ."

"Nor I," said Sab, picking his way carefully past little heaps of beast poo and crawling up a beam to his perch in the rafters. "This is a gross infringement of my griffinal liberties. I want to speak to my lawyer."

"Shut *up*," hissed Signora Strega-Borgia. "I'll try to sneak out with some supper when the mob outside has stopped baying for your blood, but until then, you might have a think about how we're supposed to compensate Mr. Pylum-Haight for the loss of his car *and* find a new home to fit all of us, when all we can afford is a small bungalow."

"But . . . aren't we going home soon?" Ffup said. "Back to our dungeon and our lovely lochside?"

"No, we are not," said Signora Strega-Borgia. "We are never going home again. StregaSchloss is ruined. From now on, we're going to live normally, in a little house with two garages, a garden shed, and a vegetable patch and garden that would probably fit into the larder at StregaSchloss. And when we look out of our windows, all that we'll be able to see is thousands of houses just like ours. Won't that be nice?"

"Waughhhhh!" howled Tock, burying his snout in a pile of straw. "I bet crocs aren't allowed anywhere near there."

"Can't imagine dragons would be too popular, either," said Ffup, his wings drooping in dejection.

"I could always turn myself back to stone and be your garden statue. Stone griffins are all the rage now," said Sab, desperately clutching at straws.

"And me," added Knot. "I'll be . . . um . . ." His yeti's imagination failed him utterly.

"The doormat," said Signora Strega-Borgia, stifling a sob. "You can be the unhygienic doormat, pet." Unable to continue without bursting into tears, she waved a goodbye and shut the stable-block door behind her.

In the darkness, the beasts huddled together for warmth and comfort. Never go back to StregaSchloss? The prospect was the stuff of nightmares. Tears trickled down fur, scales, and hide as the beasts contemplated a future that offered them no prospect of joy whatsoever.

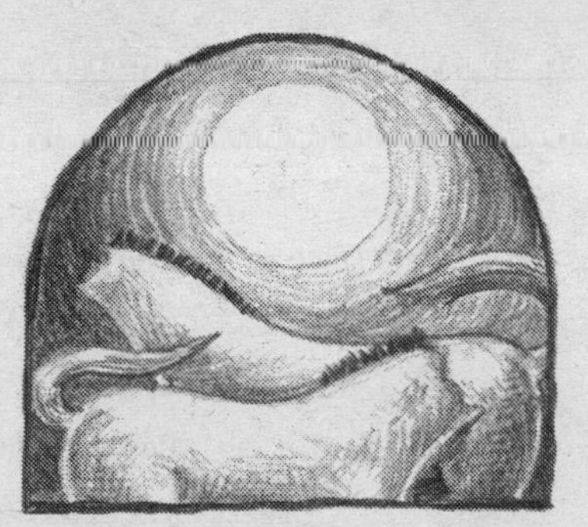

Bogginview

Following the depressing news about their ancestral home, the Strega-Borgias had grown steadily more haunted and snappy; the adults because of the impending specter of homelessness, and the children due to the sheer exhaustion experienced when looking after the needs of four hundred and four clones.

By complete contrast, the clones thrived. Their pink cheeks grew rosier, their bald heads sprouted hair, and their earlier hissing turned to cheerful clucking sounds.

"Why do they *do* that?" Pandora muttered, scraping clone poo off the bedside table for the twelfth time that morning. "That stupid *hiss-hiss, cluck-cluck* sound? It drives me insane."

"I think it's because some goose blood got into the mix when they were being made." Titus plucked an errant clone off the curtain rail, from which vantage point it had been dangling, intermittently clucking and sticking its tongue out at him.

"Get down, you little horror." Pandora dragged a particularly determined clone off the bathroom cabinet and flung it on the bed.

"*Gently,*" advised Titus. "If you damage it, I'll have to put it out of its misery, and I don't know if I'm up for that. . . ."

"This is just a total nightmare. Keeping them hidden from Latch is awful—you don't think he's caught on, do you?"

"Not yet, but he's getting pretty fed up with wearing the same clothes every day, since I 'lost' the key to the built-in wardrobe."

"What about the hissing?"

"I told him it was the central heating on the blink, but the clucking is making him a bit suspicious."

"We *can't* go on, Titus." Pandora flung herself on her brother's bed and immediately a dozen clones climbed up the bedspread and swarmed over her legs. She flapped them away halfheartedly. "Get lost, would you? Titus, when are they going to be house-trained? This is too much. *Stop* it!"

"It's just trying to be affectionate," Titus explained. "Aaah, look, it's cuddling your leg. Um . . . no, no, it's not, Pandora, I was wrong—it's peed down your trousers."

"Bummer," groaned Pandora non-anatomically. "Pass me the toilet paper." She picked the offending clone up in one hand and waggled her index finger in its face. The clone was a Pandora type and, at approximately thirty-nine years old, it stood about four inches high. "Don't. Do. That. Again," Pandora enunciated. "Use. The. Toilet. Oh, eurchh, why are they so stupid? Not the *floor,* the toilet, you dumb creature."

"We need to find them some clothes," said Titus, gazing in

horror at a Titus type that had managed to wedge a tender portion of its anatomy into an electric outlet. There was a loud bang, a thwarted hiss, and the clone's corpse fell smoking onto the carpet.

"Oh, *dear,*" said Pandora insincerely, "what a shame, only four hundred and three left. . . ."

Downstairs, in his bedroom on the fourth floor, Signor Strega-Borgia picked up the telephone and stared at it as if he feared it might sprout fangs, leap onto his neck, and bleed him dry. In the adjacent bathroom, his wife and youngest daughter were sharing a morning bath, a ritual that never failed to cheer them both up whilst simultaneously flooding the bathroom floor. The sound of running water masked the sound of Luciano Strega-Borgia taking the first steps toward selling StregaSchloss.

The day before, both he and his wife had taken a taxi back to their beloved house to view the damage for themselves. Not daring to venture inside, they had huddled in the rose garden, sheltering from the wind under a sweet chestnut tree. Tears had rolled down Signor Strega-Borgia's nose as he patted the tree trunk. "My great-grandmother planted this," he said mournfully, "and my great-grandfather planted her underneath it. . . ."

Signora Strega-Borgia looked up at the windows on the first floor. "Titus was born in the blue room," she whispered. "Do you remember? You were in such a panic. . . ."

"Second window on the right," sniffed Signor Strega-Borgia. "How could I forget? I jumped out of it and ran to find the midwife. Didn't think to use the telephone."

"Oh, Luciano," sobbed Signora Strega-Borgia, "I feel so . . . adrift without StregaSchloss. I just can't imagine how we'll ever get over losing it. I can't bear it."

"We still have our family," said Signor Strega-Borgia, hunting in his pockets for a handkerchief. "We'll always have our memories of life here."

"Damp won't remember it at all." Signora Strega-Borgia produced an unused diaper from her handbag and offered it to her husband.

The wind howled around them, shaking the naked branches of the chestnut tree and flattening the grass in the meadow. Signor Strega-Borgia shivered. "Let's go, Baci. We have to leave—the taxi has its meter running and the children will wonder where we are."

Hand in hand, each bidding an unspoken farewell to StregaSchloss, they crossed the rose garden and walked slowly back to where the waiting taxi was parked on the front drive. Little flakes of snow began to fall from the darkening sky, blown into their faces by the unforgiving wind. . . .

Recalled to the present by the dial tone changing to an automated voice reminding him to replace the handset, Signor Strega-Borgia keyed in several numbers and waited. On the other end, the phone was picked up.

"May I speak to Mr. Bella-Vista?" Signor Strega-Borgia said in a voice hardly louder than a whisper.

"One moment, please, I'll go and see if he's available to take your call. And you are . . . ?" Vadette was in full-on receptionist mode, back refreshed from the Christmas holiday.

"Luciano Strega-Borgia."

"Oh, hello there. I thought I recognized that voice. I'm quite sure Vincent would be delighted to have a word. . . ."

Depressed beyond belief, Signor Strega-Borgia listened to the retreating *tippy-tap* of Vadette's stilettos as she rushed away to give Vincent the good news. In the bathroom, a series of squeaks and squeals signaled that Damp was practicing the baby-whale impersonations that she'd perfected in the vast family bathroom at StregaSchloss. Since she was currently attempting them in a niggardly hotel bath little larger than a sink, the resulting deluge hit the floor with a loud slap. There came a pause, presumably while Damp peered over the rim of the bath to view the damage, then another splash and a squeak as she returned to her game.

"Mr. Strega-Borgia? Vincent Bella-Vista here. What can I do you for?"

The telephone felt hot in Signor Strega-Borgia's hand. In fact, the entire hotel room closed in on him suffocatingly as he sat with the receiver clutched in his hand. Feeling distinctly nauseous, he loosened his tie (a Christmas present from Mrs. McLachlan) and began to speak. On the other end of the phone, Vincent tucked the receiver under his chin and gave his girlfriend the double thumbs-up.

Shortly after lunch, the clan Strega-Borgia (minus the disgraced beasts) climbed into a taxi headed for the Bogginview estate. Mrs. McLachlan and Latch waved them off from the front steps of the hotel. The nanny folded her arms and sighed. "Oh, dear. This is not a happy time for us all."

"I loved that house," said Latch. "I can't quite imagine being a Bogginbutler, somehow."

"We must remember that it's the family who employs us and to whom we owe our loyalties, not StregaSchloss." Mrs.

McLachlan watched as the taxi disappeared where the drive wound round a curve of depressed yews. Taking Latch's arm, she turned to go back into the hotel. From her position behind the curtains in the lounge bar, Mrs. Fforbes-Campbell regarded them both with unalloyed loathing.

"Just pull over here," Signor Strega-Borgia said to the taxi driver. "We'll walk for a little bit."

Outside the warmth of the taxi, the air was bitterly cold. Mutinously, Titus and Pandora followed in their parents' wake. They'd had to jam all the clones into the wardrobes in both their bedrooms and pray that neither Latch nor Mrs. McLachlan felt a pressing need for an afternoon nap whilst they were away from the hotel. The whole operation had ensured that both children had been well and truly watered in clone pee, and in the arctic wind that whistled round Bogginview, their damp clothes clung icily to their legs.

"What a dump," moaned Titus as he stomped alongside his sister.

"The view is truly boggin," agreed Pandora. "I mean, *look* at it. I didn't know there was a swamp in Auchenlochtermuchty. . . ."

On either side of the road, dispirited little pines were blown almost parallel to the rutted soil in which they'd been planted. A sign in front of them read:

WELCOME TO BOGGINVIEW
HOMES OF THE FUTURE
ANOTHER QUALITY PROJECT FROM BELLA-VISTA

"What were the other ones?" Titus wondered out loud. "Alcatraz? The Lyubianka? Carstairs?"

"Probably," agreed Pandora. "D'you think we'll take to wearing balls and chains and nifty little suits with stripes all over them?"

The first of the "homes of the future" loomed in front of them, unfortunately sited in a rutted depression. The surrounding land was flooded with brown snowmelt in which floated several beer cans.

"Mmm, lovely," muttered Titus. "*Love* the garden."

"Water feature," corrected Pandora.

As they approached, the front door blew open to reveal Vincent Bella-Vista waving a welcome. "Mind how you go," he yelled over the howl of the wind. "It's a bit muddy. Wouldn't want you to spoil the carpets."

Huddled in their coats, the Strega-Borgias picked their way across the floodplain, wiped their feet on the doormat, and crowded into the hall of what appeared to be the Bogginview showhouse.

The builder ushered them into a tiny room that had been wallpapered within an inch of its life. The Strega-Borgias sat, squeezed into the overstuffed furniture, smiling politely and trying hard not to stare at the carpet (white), the chandelier (hung so low that its bottom dangly bits scraped the coffee table), the colossal television (on, with sound turned off), and the vast picture (white horses dancing on a moonlit beach) that dominated the mantelpiece.

"Home, sweet home," said the builder, unwittingly expressing the exact opposite of what the Strega-Borgias were unanimously thinking. Damp slid off her father's knee and patted the carpet tentatively.

"Right, folks." In the absence of any encouraging cues from the family, Vincent Bella-Vista shifted gear. "Let's have a look round. See what you think. Let the kiddies get their bearings."

The kiddies stared back at him with flat alien eyes. Such was the combined effect of their glare that the builder flailed, faltered, and entered the verbal equivalent of a wheel spin: "Er. Yes. So. Um. If you'll just follow me. . . . Here we have the fully fitted kitchen-cum-dining room. . . ."

Waiting till Mr. Bella-Vista and the Strega-Borgias had squeezed out of the living room, Pandora unscrewed the lid on her tub of vanishing cream and made some adjustments to the picture hanging over the mantelpiece. *Perfect,* she thought, turning to rejoin her family; here we have the little-known masterpiece—White *Head*less Horses Dancing on a Moonlit Beach. Trying to appear interested in Mr. Bella-Vista's monologue, she crept into the kitchen as the builder continued.

". . . and on this wall, we have the built-in-microwave-deep-fat-frier-indoor-barbecue-dishwasher-garbage-disp—"

It was just at this moment, as the hapless Vincent Bella-Vista was extolling the virtues of his all-electric house, that Auchenlochtermuchty suffered a total power cut.

The Beastly Blues

Unaware that the world around them had been plunged into midwinter twilight, the beasts had been digging an escape tunnel by Braille. Earlier that afternoon, they'd come to a unanimous decision to run away, since their future in a Bogginview bungalow seemed fraught with difficulties. Incorrectly assuming that they were unloved since the BMW-torching episode, they put an escape plan into operation. They toyed with the idea of burning down the locked stable door with dragon flame, or simply smashing it to smithereens by beast power, but after much debate, they decided that digging their way out would give them several hours of freedom before anyone noticed that they'd gone. Several hours later, a vast mound of recently dug earth towered over the tunnel, round which Sab, Ffup, and Knot stood whispering words of encouragement down to Tock.

"Can't see a thing," muttered the crocodile, his front paws sending up a continual shower of earth and pebbles.

"D'you need a break?" said Ffup, looking up from manicuring his talons. "Shall I warm your poor wee paws up a bit?"

"No, thank you," said Tock. "Crispy claws are not my idea of a helpful suggestion."

"What happens when we're out?" demanded Sab. "Has anyone thought that far ahead? Then what? Where do we go from here?"

"Back home," sniffed the dragon. "Back to our lovely dungeon. I'll get a fire going, you catch us some grub. . . ."

"I don't eat meat," Tock reminded them, in between pawfuls of grassy earth.

"We'll find you some winter greens in the kitchen garden, then," said Ffup, "and then . . . well, we'll just have to be self-sufficient, won't we?"

"DONE IT!" yelled Tock. "We're FREE!"

Freezing air poured in through the escape tunnel as the beasts hurriedly packed their meager possessions and headed for the wide-open spaces of the Auchenlochtermuchty Arms parking lot. The recent power cut had worked to their advantage, as all the street lamps were temporarily extinguished. Tock led his co-conspirators toward the river, which flowed in the direction of Lochnagargoyle, the sea loch overlooked by StregaSchloss. The beasts followed a circuitous route through Auchenlochtermuchty, emerging at last into the fields that marked the outskirts of the village. Spattered with mud and chilled to the marrow, they began to wonder if they'd Done The Right Thing.

They stood in a huddle at the edge of a turnip field and tried to get their bearings.

"What's that *shhhlepp shhhlepp* noise?" whispered Sab, clutching the dragon's arm. "It's coming closer now. Can you hear it?"

"I think it's me," admitted Knot, stopping in his tracks and sitting down abruptly. "It's my fur, dragging through the mud."

"Where *are* we?" wailed Ffup. "I don't recognize any of this. . . ." Over their heads, a pitiless December sky stretched blackly in all directions.

"I smell something," said Sab.

"I think it's me," confessed Knot. "It usually is. . . ."

"No, it's not you, this time." The griffin sniffed loudly, his curved nostrils expanding alarmingly. "It's more like raw lamb. . . ."

Borne on the wind toward where they stood shivering was an unmistakable *baa-baa*.

"Did you hear that?" Sab nudged Ffup. "Meals-on-hooves sort of sound?"

"I always did prefer my lamb underdone," mused Ffup. "Two minutes each side. . . ."

"No meat for me," Tock reminded them.

"Oh, quit being so picky, would you? If we were stranded on a desert island, you'd soon learn to eat meat again."

"I'd rather starve."

"The way I see it, my stubborn friend," said Ffup, wrapping a wing around the sulking crocodile and drawing him to one side, "is that you have some tough choices up ahead. You can join me and the boys as we pick ourselves some free-range lamb, or, as you said, you can starve . . . or"—the dragon indicated the vast expanse of field ahead of them—"you could dine in style on raw muddy turnips. What's it to be?"

Tock weighed the options open to him and sighed. "I suppose if you cook meat for me, it would be rude to refuse."

"Come on then. Let's go get them!" And with a ponderous flap of his leathery wings, Ffup took to the skies, followed by Sab.

The moon came out from behind a bank of snow clouds and cast their twin wheeling shadows into sharp relief against the frozen ruts of the field below. Following behind, awkwardly earthbound, came Knot and Tock, stumbling over turnips and breaking through the icy crust on the occasional puddle. The *baa-baa* sound came closer and louder now. Dinner was growing nervous.

Clones on the Rampage

Shrouded in gloom, the Strega-Borgias returned to the hotel in Vincent Bella-Vista's white van. The journey proved to be a singularly unpleasant one due to the odor emanating from dozens of discarded Styrofoam containers, whose decomposing contents bore witness to the builder's fondness for beefburgers and his inability to finish anything he started. Attempting to make conversation with Vincent Bella-Vista, Signor Strega-Borgia found a tiny bit of common ground between Bogginview and StregaSchloss.

"Your chandelier . . . ," he began, "reminded me of the one at StregaSchloss. . . . Of course, ours is an ancient old thing, been hanging there for about four hundred years. . . ."

Vincent Bella-Vista yawned widely, and grunted to indicate that he was listening.

Signor Strega-Borgia continued, "D'you know, I've often wondered if the legend of the Borgia Diamond is true. . . ."

Sitting next to his father, Titus groaned. Not *that* old thing again. Boring, boring, boring. He rolled his eyes at Pandora as their father droned on.

". . . apparently, or so I was told by my grandfather, one of the crystal teardrops on our chandelier is rumored to be a diamond, hidden up there by a long-dead relative, Malvolio di S'Enchantedino Borgia, during the Mhoire Ochone Uprising of . . . um . . . er . . ."

"Sixteen forty-eight," muttered Signora Strega-Borgia, adding, "Or so they *say*. Honestly, darling, if it were true, we would hardly be about to sell StregaSchloss to Mr. Belle Atavista here, would we? We'd be selling the diamond and using the proceeds to mend our poor . . . our lovely . . . oh, Lucianoooo." She stopped, tears spilling down her face.

At this unhappy moment, the van's headlights picked out the profile of the Auchenlochtermuchty Arms, wreathed in fog and, regrettably, still without electricity. On the desk in the reception area, an oil lamp threw just enough light to enable the family to pick their way to the residents' lounge. To Titus and Pandora's relief, sitting on either side of a blazing fire were Latch and Mrs. McLachlan, deep in the final stages of a game of Monopoly, which, judging by the number of houses and hotels littering the board, had been going on all afternoon. This fireside cameo was so reminiscent of rainy winter days spent in the library at StregaSchloss that the family felt their bleak mood recede slightly.

Signor Strega-Borgia moved a chair closer to the fire. Maybe it might be possible to re-create some of the ambience, if not the identical surroundings of StregaSchloss, he thought, staring into the flames.

If we got rid of that ghastly carpet and brought some of our own books and paintings, perhaps even Bogginview could become a home for us all, thought Signora Strega-Borgia, curling onto a sofa.

No such domestic concerns entered the heads of Titus and Pandora. Their shared preoccupation was with the clones and what had happened in their caretakers' absence. Excusing themselves, they made for the stairs.

Four flights up, they found an abandoned flashlight lying in an alcove. As Titus turned it on, its beam swept across the cobwebby ceiling, causing Pandora to be struck by an unhappy thought.

"Tarantella . . . ," she moaned, grabbing Titus's arm. "If there's no roof left at StregaSchloss, then there's no attic, either. Oh, poor her. . . ." She slumped against the wall and groaned.

"Come on," Titus sighed. "Never mind that horrible tarantula, we have to deal with the clones."

"*Your* clones," said Pandora, following reluctantly upstairs. "*My* spider. I didn't get us into this mess, Titus."

"Help me out here, would you?" said Titus. "We'll try and hide the clones somewhere no one can hear them and then, I promise, I'll come back to StregaSchloss with you and we'll find your spider."

"And Multitudina and Terminus?"

"You drive a hard bargain, but yes, them, too."

They stopped outside Titus's room. Filtered through the door came music and voices. Little voices. Lots of them. Titus unlocked the door and edged in, followed by Pandora.

A scene of chaos and mayhem greeted them. The clones, mercifully no larger than earlier that day, but regrettably far more vocal, were backlit by Titus's laptop. Absorbed in their own world, they failed to notice the arrival of their giant caretakers.

"They must have broken out of the wardrobe . . . and where did they get that music?" Pandora whispered.

"It's a CD. They're playing it on my laptop, the little toads."

The little toads gyrated, bumped, and ground to the rhythm. The fact that they were still utterly naked merely added to the overall hideousness. Out from behind the splintered door of the wardrobe came a pungent odor that suggested that though the clones may have mastered the workings of Titus's laptop, the complexities of a toilet still eluded them.

"HEY!" squeaked one of the Titus types. "It's the big dude and dudette! Come in—join the party! What took you so long?"

On the screen of the laptop, a dialogue box informed them that the laptop's battery was heading for pancake status and pretty soon the lights would dim, the music stop, and it would be time to go home. Pandora lit a candle, and in the flare of the match accidentally scorched a clone. Heartlessly running it under the bathroom tap and telling it to quit moaning, she headed back into the bedroom and clapped her hands for attention.

"RIGHT, YOU LOT," she said in a voice learned firsthand from Mrs. McLachlan, "enough of this nonsense. Turn that racket off, go and wash your faces, and then it's time for bed."

A communal "Awwww" went up from the clones. Mutters of "That's not fair" and "Boring" were ignored as the tribe of clones trooped obediently into the bathroom.

Titus was seriously impressed. His immediate response to the sight of the clone revel was to lie down on the carpet and sob, but his sister had managed to get the situation under control in one minute flat.

"Right, Titus," she said, still in McLachlan mode, "you supervise face washing and I'll go and find somewhere for them to sleep." Placing the candle on her brother's bedside table, she tiptoed out into the corridor. A dim light filtered up from downstairs as she groped her way along the landing. Encountering one of the many vast radiators that normally hissed and bubbled all night long, she noticed that it was stone cold. Opposite the radiator, the door to the linen cupboard stood open. Reaching inside, Pandora helped herself to a large pile of woollen blankets and continued on her passage down the darkened landing. Just as she was about to give up and try another floor, she saw the perfect solution to the clone-containment problem. A hatch halfway up the wall proclaimed itself to be a service lift. On the brass plate engraved with this information were two unlit buttons and a small notice that read:

STAFF ONLY
IN THE EVENT OF A POWER FAILURE, PLEASE USE THE MANUAL PULLEY

The service lift must have stopped somewhere between floors when the power cut occurred. Sure that even the most determined clones couldn't break out of what was, in effect, a ventilated metal safe, Pandora opened the hatch and peered inside. In the darkness, she made out a brass wheel roughly the size of a dinner plate. She groped in the dark and began to turn the wheel clockwise. From far below her feet, a distant rumble told her that the lift was on its way.

Meanwhile, Titus had raided both Latch's and his own

supply of socks in order to provide some of the clones with a rudimentary form of clothing to protect them from the ravages of a Scottish winter in a currently unheated hotel. Using the butler's toenail clippers, Titus gouged a neck hole in the toe of each sock, shredded two armholes in either side, and dragged the woolly tubes over the protesting heads of as many clones as he could find socks for. Turning his attention to the remainder of the naked clones, who huddled shivering on his bed, he began to cut a hotel towel into tiny squares and, with a hole chewed in the center of each square, managed to clothe the sockless clones in tiny toweling ponchos. Ignoring their protests of "I'm not wearing *that*" and "I want an *Adidas* sock, not a boring old woolly one," Titus stuffed the last Titus type back into the sock from which it had been trying to escape and sat down abruptly on the floor.

He was *exhausted*. Around him, sock- and poncho-clad clones yawned and whined incessantly, their twitching bodies casting giant candlelit shadows on the wall behind them.

Titus was nearly asleep when Pandora poked her head round the door and beckoned him over. "We'll have to do this in batches," she said. "How many d'you think we can carry at a time?"

"No more than ten."

"That won't work. It would take us all night. . . ." Pandora looked at the herds of clones lolling on Titus's bed, comparing socks and ponchos.

"The bedspread," Titus said. "We can bundle them all up in it and carry them in one go."

The clones were less than keen on this plan for their travel arrangements. Bundled ignominiously into a candlewick bedspread and then dragged bumpily along the corridor, they protested loudly. At the end of the corridor, the service lift yawned open. Pandora had carefully lined its floor with blankets to deaden the noise and to provide some insulation against the chill of the metal lift. Such thoughtfulness failed to impress the clones. Their protests became more shrill as Titus and Pandora heaved the candlewick bundle into the empty lift.

"Oh, do shut *up,*" said Pandora, slamming the door on their howls of outrage and beginning to turn the wheel. The noise diminished with each turn until, finally giving it four complete turns for good measure, Pandora closed the hatch and slumped against the wall. Downstairs, the clock in reception chimed eight o'clock. Dinnertime. "I'll meet you by the front door at midnight," she said. "And pray that the power stays off till then."

"There are some advantages to having no electricity." Titus grinned. "I can guarantee that there will be no Brussels sprouts with dinner. . . ."

Brief Encounter

Sheltered under a clump of Scots pines, the beasts gazed up at the moonlit sky in a state of utter contentment. Earlier, Ffup had lit a small fire and they had roasted their dinner over the flames. Sab idly scanned the loch shore for perfectly flat skimming stones. Tock grinned widely, unaware that his many teeth were speckled with the burnt remains of barbecued mutton. He patted his stomach, tossed a large bone into the fire, and flopped back against a tree trunk.

Ffup regarded him balefully. "I must say, for a reluctant convert to carnivorism, you choked down far more than your fair share. . . ."

The crocodile nodded in agreement. He had devoured the best part of one entire sheep, leaving only the back legs for his companions. Disgusted, Ffup stood up and turned round to warm his wings at the fire. Overhead, clouds scudded across the winter sky. The beasts shivered and drew closer to the flames. Far away, something howled.

"What was *that*?" Sab's voice shook.

Knot looked up from a half-gnawed leg bone. Grease had dribbled down his front, adding to his perpetually unsavory appearance, and clots of semi-masticated mutton dotted his tangled fur. "Maybe a wolf?" he mumbled hopefully. "D'you think they'd taste good?"

"I'll go and investigate," said Ffup. "You guys stay here and keep the fire going. I'll be back in a moment."

Stepping out from the shelter of the pines, he stretched his wings to their full span and, with a couple of languid flaps, disappeared over the treetops.

Sab looked around. Tock was sprawled beside the fire emitting a loud reptilian snore, punctuated with occasional belches as he digested his dinner. The griffin threw another log on the fire and stared into the flames.

"Reminds me of being a toddler," he said, his eyes misting over with the effort of recalling events from four centuries past. "We were sharing a roost with Ffup's family in the Great Forest of Caledon. . . . Ffup's dad had been forcibly relocated there after a bit of an upset over exceeding his quota of edible maidens. . . . Ffup's mum had a broken wing. . . ." He paused to check that he had the yeti's undivided attention and continued. "Anyway, Malvolio di S'Enchantedino Borgia, who'd evicted some dodgy tenant from StregaSchloss, had installed his ancient grandmother in his wine cellar—and she was totally batty, gray hair down to her knees—called Strega-Nonna. . . . Stop me if you've heard this before, won't you?"

The yeti smiled politely and crammed another lump of sheepskin into his glistening maw. Knot had heard this story a thousand times or more, but in the absence of their beloved StregaSchloss, it was somehow comforting to recall the house, even if only in the form of legend. Knot settled down in the pine needles, his body language indicating his willingness to have the griffin continue. Sparks flew into the darkness, and above the hiss from the fire came the howl again, fainter now.

Much later, as Sab had reached the interesting bit about how Strega-Nonna had mended his mother's wing with a combination of magic and cobwebs, a leathery flapping sound alerted the beasts to the return of Ffup. The dragon swooped down onto the carpet of pine needles and stood, towering above them, wings slowly folding back against his spine, his scales in some disarray. "Heavens! Is that the time? I'd no idea I'd been away for so long."

The beasts regarded their colleague in some confusion. Ffup babbled on, blissfully unaware. "Amazing how time flies when you're having fun. Who'd have thought it? After all these years of snorting and spitting and trying to be pure dead macho. . . . And then, tonight, on this gloriously romantic winter night, something . . . *something* showed me my true female nature. Guys, guess what, I'm a girl—" The dragon stopped in mid-babble, arrested by the faint but unmistakable sound of a distant howl.

"Ffup? FFUP!" Sab hugged the dragon and lifted up his . . . no—*her* chin in order to stare into her eyes. "Ffup? You're . . . you're . . ."

"WHAT?" squeaked the dragon, unaccustomed to being the center of attention and trying desperately to bury her head in her wings.

"You're *blushing*!"

The Guilt Trip

Titus's feet were freezing. He'd donated every pair of socks that he possessed in the pursuit of clone clothing, and this left him with no other option but to wear wellies over his bare feet as he and his sister walked to their old home. And, he realized, he was developing blisters on both heels.

"Stop sulking, Titus," said Pandora. "I did my bit to help with the clones; now it's your turn to reciprocate with finding Tarantella."

Behind them, the lights of Auchenlochtermuchty suddenly came back on. They twinkled reassuringly in the dark, offering Titus and Pandora no comfort whatsoever.

"The *lift,*" moaned Pandora, struck by the implications of a full return to normal electric supplies. "It'll start working."

"Just hurry up," muttered Titus. "The sooner we get this over and done with, the sooner we can deal with the clones."

Stumbling and moaning, they half-ran, half-walked till they

reached the main gate to StregaSchloss. The sign that warned trespassers that they would be eaten for breakfast/turned into frogs/forced to eat Brussels sprouts was completely obscured by a police notice that read:

WARNING—HAZARDOUS BUILDING
no entry except by authorized personnel

Disregarding this, the children scrambled over the gate and stopped for a moment, drinking in the sight of their old home. Silhouetted in the moonlight, StregaSchloss stood before them, its exposed roof timbers skeletal and derelict against the night sky.

"Oh, poor *house,*" whispered Pandora, horrified at the extent of the damage.

Titus groaned in agreement. "They'll *never* fix it now. It's a wreck."

As they ran toward home, they couldn't fail to notice further signs of dilapidation. Tock's moat had overflowed its boundaries, spilling mud across the rose-quartz courtyard. An overturned wheelie bin had vomited its contents across the kitchen garden and shredded plastic bags had wrapped themselves round an ancient wisteria, flapping and rattling in the wind that scoured the south-facing wall.

Something was wrong with the drains as well. . . . When Titus and Pandora lifted the stone griffin that both guarded the front door and provided a handy stash for the key, their bent heads were brought into close proximity to a covered drain.

"Phwoarrr!" Titus reeled back in disgust. "And I thought

rancid goose was the pits. . . ." He pulled the collar of his fleece up over his nose and mouth and unlocked the front door. They pushed past a soggy pile of leaves that had gathered in the doorway in their absence and, at last, returned to their true home.

The sight that greeted them was the antithesis of a homecoming. Shining through the stained-glass windows of the first-floor landing, the moon illuminated a StregaSchloss abandoned, desolate, and, to the children's eyes, wounded beyond hope of recovery. The very air was damp with the kind of sepulchral chill that invited one not to linger overlong. Furthermore, it stank, as if some creature had crawled into the plumbing system to die.

Titus flicked a switch, with little hope. To his surprise, the lights came on overhead. "Right, Pan, where first?"

"Let's try the kitchen. Multitudina might be holed up in the pantry."

Clutching each other for comfort, they crept along the passage to the kitchen, each of them secretly holding out little hope of finding anything left alive.

"Multitudina . . . ?" whispered Pandora, reaching out to turn on the light.

From the depths of the kitchen range came an exasperated "*Tchhhh.* Totally typical," said a familiar voice. "She returns after an extended absence and her first words are not 'Oh, Tarantella, oh, great mother-of-millions, oh, faithful, intelligent, beautiful Tarantella, how ever can I make it up to you?' Hah. NOT. 'Oh, dear Tarantella—by the way, happy belated Christmas from your adoring Pandora.' Hah. NOT.

'Oh, forgive me, faithless, heartless biped wretch that I am. . . .' "

"Okay—*enough,*" sighed Pandora. "Sorry. I am sorry. Very."

"That's simply not good enough." Tarantella glared through the air vent at Pandora and folded all eight legs into a huffy bundle. "Come *on.* Increase the sincerity factor, up the emotional content, and SAY IT LIKE YOU REALLY MEAN IT!"

Pandora burst into tears. As if it wasn't bad enough returning to your wrecked home, being lectured by an invisible tarantula put the lid on it. "I'm really, really SORRY!" she bawled. "All RIGHT? I'm utterly miserable—you've no idea how horrible all this is. . . ." She became incoherent with grief, leaning on Titus for support.

"Awwwk. Don't *leak* like that, girl." Tarantella slipped through the air vent and waved a hairy leg at the children. "Oh, lordy, I see you've brought your arachnophobic sibling, too. What joy. . . ."

In the harsh electric light, Titus saw that the whole kitchen was festooned with cobwebs. Seeing him gazing at her handiwork, Tarantella shrugged. "A girl has to keep busy, you know. Make some attempt to draft-proof this dingy hole. It was so gloomy here, as I'm *sure* you can imagine. . . . No lights, no crackling log fires, no Christmas tree, no—"

"Sultana," came a hoarse whisper from the pantry.

"*Santa,* you moron," Tarantella snapped, continuing, "Bleak and cheerless, no presents, no Christmas cards, no—"

"Dirty raisins," added Multitudina, emerging from hiding.

"Oh, give me strength," moaned Tarantella. "DECORATIONS, not 'dirty raisins.' Are you completely illiterate or what?"

Multitudina sniffed huffily and scuttled down the stairs to the dungeons, yelling backward over her shoulder, "YES I AM! I'm an ILLITERAT! I was brought up to EAT books, not READ them. . . ."

The Unspeakable Pursue the Inedible

Loud clankings and rumbles woke the clones from their candlewick-entangled slumbers. As electricity surged round Auchenlochtermuchty, it caused the service lift to drop swiftly down the shaft and clang to a halt at kitchen level. The clones pressed forward, tripping over socks and ponchos and bruising several of their fellow incubatees in the process. The hatch opened and a reek of stale whisky breath washed over them. Mortimer stood before them, weaving slightly and muttering to himself.

"What does she take me for, eh? Bally laundry maid, what? Chap like me shouldn't have to do this. Women's work, what? Frightful inconvenience. . . ."

Grumbling drunkenly, he grabbed the candlewick bedspread and staggered across the kitchen to the laundry area. With a loud hiccup, he stuffed the bedspread, clones and all, into the hotel's colossal industrial washer-dryer. "Must lay off the sauce,

Mortimer, old bean," he advised himself. "Beginning to hear the voices again, what?"

He sprinkled the alarmed clones with washing powder, threw a jugful of fabric conditioner in for good measure, and then paused, his liver-spotted hands trembling over the ON switch. "Hands gone all wobbly, what?" he observed, holding them up to his face to inspect them. "All four of them, shaking like reeds. Come to think of it, Mortimer, old stick, what's the world coming to when a chap can't keep track of his own limbs, what? Myself, I blame the present government, actually. . . ."

Muttering incoherently, he spun round several times, reached into the depths of the broom cupboard, and produced a bottle of Old Liverot—a singularly foul malt whisky whose only virtue was its strength. Weaving more noticeably, Mortimer clutched this bottle to his chest and lurched out of the laundry area, fortunately forgetting to turn on the washer-dryer.

The brief shower of fabric conditioner had done nothing to improve the clones' tempers, and they swarmed out of the washing machine, sleep-deprived, speckled with washing powder, and intent on revenge. At that moment Beelzebub, resident cat of the Auchenlochtermuchty Arms, poked his scarred nose through his cat flap into the kitchen. Years of guerilla warfare in the village alleyways had taught him to be ever vigilant and, if in doubt, to turn tail and run. He spotted movement over by the washing machine and, whiskers twitching, crept silently through the cat flap in order to investigate. The sight of so many shrunken humans pouring across the tiles caused him to panic. Beelzebub instantly inflated himself into something akin to an orange toilet brush, flattened his ears back against his skull, and gave what he fervently hoped was a fearsome growl.

The clones were not impressed by this. However, bored by their sartorial range being confined to Latch and Titus's socks and towels, they were seriously impressed by the colorful nature of Beelzebub's fur. "Cool," a Titus type yelled. "Hey, you guys, let's get ourselves some new orange threads."

Beelzebub took one horrified look at the advancing hordes of tiny figures and, skidding inelegantly on the tiles, spun right round and bolted out of the cat flap.

The clones were not to be put off that easily. Brandishing Latch's toenail clippers like a battering ram, they didn't pause to draw up a battle plan. With the massed howl of hundreds of thwarted fashion victims, they set off in pursuit.

Beelzebub ran for his life. Whatever the mysteriously shrunken humans were, the cat was sure they didn't have his future welfare in mind. He paused for breath on the outskirts of the village, turning round to see how far behind his pursuers were.

Behind him, in a seething horde, the clones sprinted along the main road, their lamplit shadows forming and reforming as they crossed from one pool of light to the next. Wondering if the shrunken ones could climb trees, Beelzebub headed for the uncharted territory of the track to StregaSchloss, hoping to find shelter in the bramble jungle that arched over his head. Nearly prostrate with terror, the cat squeezed through a thicket and scrabbled up the trunk of an ivy-clad oak. Out of breath, he perched on a lofty branch and peered down into the darkness below to see what the clones would make of this new development.

He didn't have long to wait. Undaunted by the dangers of the bramble thorns, the clones clustered round the base of Beelzebub's tree. They spotted their prey instantly and began to climb up the ivy.

When the first wave of poncho-clad clones reached Beelzebub's perch, the cat edged backward till he was in danger of running out of branch. Beneath his weight the branch sagged ominously.

"Cool color," remarked one Pandora type, imagining herself clad in Beelzebub's fur. "I want that bit with the white stripes. . . ."

Beelzebub sprang for safety, leaping across the gap into the branches of an adjoining oak. The effect of this was to make the branch he'd just vacated spring whippily into the air and dislodge all the clambering clones. A flock of ponchos billowed merrily into the night, and then, obeying the dictates of gravity, fluttered downward, coming to a jerky halt as the bramble thorns caught in the toweling fabric, leaving the clones dangling from the branches, arms and legs waving helplessly in the air.

Their companions regrouped at the foot of the tree in a state of shock. Above their heads, the night was rent with loud complaints.

"Aaaargh!" shrieked a Titus type. "Get me down! I'm freezing!"

Trying to stifle her giggles, a Pandora type pulled her sock up over her head to obliterate the vision of what hung dangling overhead.

"This is a grave offense against the dignity of clonehood!"

screamed another Titus type, beating his tiny fists against the oak tree. "Orange Fur will pay dearly for this. REVENGE, my brothers and sisters, REVENGE. . . ."

Taking this as a perfect opportunity to escape, Beelzebub fled up the track, heading in the direction of StregaSchloss.

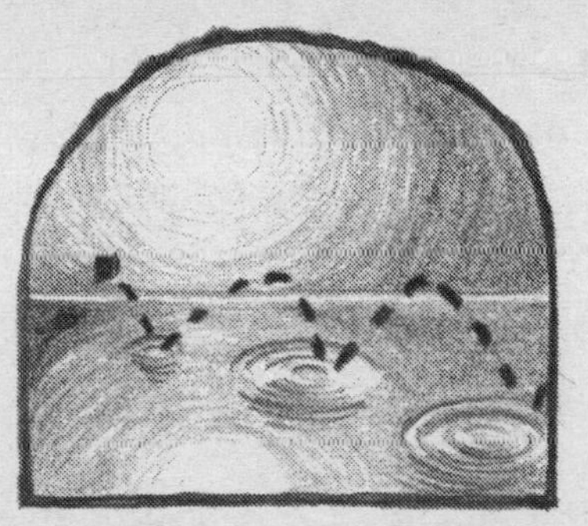

Wee Things Without Pants

"But what happened?" Knot whined. "I don't understand. No one ever tells me anything."

The beasts stood on the shore of Lochnagargoyle, within sight of home.

"D'you mean the roof?" said Sab, expertly skimming a pebble across the lapping water. "We told you. It blew off. On Christmas Eve, remember?"

"No," wailed Knot, "I don't mean the *roof*. I mean what happened to Ffup? He's—no, *she's* gone all . . . weird."

"It's a girl thing," muttered the dragon. "Don't ask."

Tock emerged from the loch, his scales dripping and his claws scrabbling for purchase on the seaweedy pebbles. "Here's another of those stones for you, Sab," he said, handing the griffin a perfectly flat and square example. "My claws are frozen stiff. If you want any more skimming stones, you'll have to get them yourself." He shivered. "Let's go back home."

"For some reason, I'm utterly famished," remarked Ffup, picking up a mouthful of seaweed and devouring it. The beasts ignored her completely. For the past half hour since the dragon had returned from her investigation into the source of the Distant Howl, she'd been acting very strangely. She was inwardly focused, vague, giggly, and perpetually complaining about how hungry she was.

"Is that a light up there?" she said through another dripping mouthful of seaweed, vaguely flapping a claw in the direction of StregaSchloss. "I thought I could see a glow through the trees."

The beasts stood on the loch shore, peering through the night at their old home. There *was* a light. Headlights swung down the track, sweeping across the fields and throwing the skeletal shadows of trees up against the walls of StregaSchloss. Just as suddenly as they had appeared, the lights vanished and the unmistakable rattle of an approaching Land Rover stopped. To the beasts' confusion, the vehicle appeared to be creeping down the drive, lights out, engine cut, stealthily advancing toward the deserted house.

"Something's not right," said Sab, his eyes narrowing in suspicion. "Let's go and see what's going on."

The beasts tiptoed in single file, negotiating the gorse-lined path that led from the loch shore to the meadow. Now that they were closer to home, they could see that some of the house lights were on, throwing diamonds of light over the drive, across the grass, and picking out the naked branches of the chestnut tree. Desperately homesick, puzzled, and exceedingly wary, the procession of beasts halted in the meadow and waited to see if their ancestral home was under threat.

"RIGHT, YOU HORRIBLE LOT. FALL IN!"

Light shone out from the kitchen windows of StregaSchloss across the littered kitchen garden. It illuminated Signora Strega-Borgia's parsley patch, it filtered through the leaves of her bay tree, and it picked out a tiny figure perched on an upturned plant pot.

"ON THE DOUBLE! QUICK MARCH! ONE, TWO. ONE, TWO. ONE, TWO!" The tiny figure leaned on its shield and sighed in exasperation. Then it hitched up its kilt over its stomach. "PICK YOUR FEET UP, YOU MISERABLE SNIVELING WRETCHES! YOU'RE SUPPOSED TO BE AN INVINCIBLE UNIT OF THE FIFTH DRAGON'S-TOOTH ENGINEERS!! OH, GIVE ME *STRENGTH*! ABOUT TURRN! HAAAAALT!"

On the sodden ground below their bawling leader, the massed ranks of the tincture squaddies came to a mutinous standstill. Several of them tripped over their shields and fell into the parsley. Seeing this, their leader sank to his knees on the plant pot and banged his head five times against his shield. The tincture squaddies watched this performance impassively. They'd seen it all before, many times. Next, their leader would stand up, hurl more abuse at them, and begin the whole exercise again. It was the pits. The army was the pits, their leader was the pits, and this godforsaken country, with its vast parsley trees, giant marauding spiders, big rude cats, and endless snow and rain, was —

"RUBBISH!" Their leader was back on his feet again, jumping up and down on top of the plant pot. "THAT WAS RUBBISH! HAVE YOU ALL GOT CLOTH EARS OR WHAT? READ MY LIPS! FAAAAALL IN!"

They fell in. Reluctantly, grumbling about the unfairness of the fate that had brought them here to train and fight and die; moaning about the inadequacies of their uniform, given the hostile climate, they still did as they were told, and fell in.

A short distance away, separated by stone walls and panes of glass, Titus blinked. "You're kidding, right?" He sat at the kitchen table, staring open-mouthed at Tarantella.

Pandora had managed to light the fire in the range and the kitchen was growing warmer by the minute. She'd found some shriveled carrots and onions and had made a kind of vegetable soup, which she was now dishing into a bowl for Multitudina while Titus listened to Tarantella's unbelievable story.

"Have it your own way, dear boy," the spider said, pausing as she applied pink lipstick to her mouthparts. "It's a tale, told by an idiot, *sigh,* signifying noth—"

"Is it true? Come on, Tarantella, this is *important.*"

Tarantella glared at Titus, snapped the cap back onto her lipstick, and tucked it away in a hidden pouch under her abdomen. She looked up at him, smiled in a decidedly insincere fashion, and produced her comb from another pouch. Humming to herself, she began to groom her legs with maddening slowness.

Titus turned to his sister. "Help me out here, would you? Tell me, what do I have to do to get to the bottom of this story—fall to my knees on the floor and beg?"

"That would be a good start," Tarantella said. "And while you're at it, you could get me something to eat. Good flies are so hard to find these days. . . ."

"*Tarantella*"—Pandora remembered how effective McLachlan mode had been in quelling the rebellious clones—"stop messing about. Tell us what happened on Christmas Eve or I'll send you to the attic without any supper."

"Oh, *my*. Hark at it now." The tarantula hopped across the table and ran up Pandora's arm.

Titus gagged. If that hideous spider had done that to him, he'd have died on the spot.

"Such a bossy little boots," Tarantella continued, tapping Pandora's nose with a reproving hairy leg. "However, seeing as it's *you* and not him, I'll tell you." And she crawled up Pandora's hair and began whispering in her ear, "*Psss-psss* roofers, *hiss-psss* pulled slates off, *psst-hssst* lost in the loch, *pss*."

"LOCHNAGARGOYLE?" gasped Pandora, struck by the wickedness of it all. "They threw our slates in the *loch*?"

"Never to be found again," came a familiar voice from the kitchen door. "And after your unfortunate accident, that's where you're headed, too."

Swathed in golden fur and holding a gun in front of her, Ffion Fforbes-Campbell stepped into the kitchen, followed by Hugh Pylum-Haight. In the horrified silence, Tarantella scuttled unobserved out through the open kitchen door.

Rising Damp

The clatter of the Fforbes-Campbell Land Rover leaving the Auchenlochtermuchty Arms had woken Damp from a deep sleep. Rubbing her eyes with chubby fists, she assessed how exactly she felt about this. It all hinged on the status of her diaper. If it was dry and warm, nine times out of ten she'd roll over and go back to sleep, but tonight, the cold clamminess round her bottom augured ill. Damp stood up, her travel cot creaking loudly as her weight shifted. Sometimes this sound was enough to wake the sleeping mummy summit. Tonight, this was not to be. Damp cleared her throat and experimented with a Grade One Whimper. Sometimes, this was all it took. . . .

By the time Mrs. McLachlan reached her cotside, Damp had progressed to the deafening heights of Grade Eight (Full-on Sobbing with Extra Hiccups for Good Measure). The baby was so enchanted with her own operatic prowess that it was several minutes before she realized that she had an audience.

"You poor wee chook," clucked Mrs. McLachlan, scooping the tear-stained baby up into her arms for a hug. "Och, my wee lamb . . . my poor little honey-bunny, what's the matter?"

The baby gave a wail and burrowed deep into her nanny's comforting chest.

"Was it a bad dream, sweet pea?" murmured the nanny, stroking Damp's head. "Don't know *where* your parents have gone," she continued, turning on the bedside light and sitting down on Signor and Signora Strega-Borgia's empty bed with Damp on her lap. "And when I woke up, Pandora had vanished, too."

A knock came and Latch's head appeared round the door. "Flora," he whispered, rubbing his eyes, "where *is* everyone? Young Titus isn't in his bed and it's gone three a.m."

"Why don't you try downstairs?" suggested Mrs. McLachlan. "I'll come down and give you a hand just as soon as I've settled the wee one back in her cot."

Damp stiffened. Back in her cot? No way was she going back *there*. Ah, well—she was left with little choice. . . . The opening aria from Grade Nine filled the tiny hotel bedroom, beating off the walls, swelling to an ear-splitting crescendo of High-C Shrieks coupled with Progressive Choking Sounds that threatened to overwhelm both audience and performer. The audience capitulated and bore the diva downstairs. Two minutes later, their ears still ringing, Mrs. McLachlan, Latch, and Damp found one half of their missing family. In the darkened lounge bar, Signor Strega-Borgia bent over the lifeless form of Mortimer Fforbes-Campbell, while behind the bar, Signora Strega-Borgia was on the phone to the nearest hospital, explaining the nature of the emergency.

"Blue. Yes, his mouth is still blue," she said, a discernible note of panic creeping into her voice. "No. We're not sure what he's taken. Might just be the alcohol—I'm pretty positive he's had most of a bottle of whisky, but I think that's pretty normal for him. . . ."

Under the assault of Signor Strega-Borgia's vigorous chest massage, Mortimer's inert body flopped like a landed fish. Grimacing at the prospect ahead, Signor Strega-Borgia ceased his efforts at kick-starting Morty's heart and turned his attention to administering the kiss of life. He pinched the landlord's red nose between finger and thumb, waved away Latch and Mrs. McLachlan's offers of help, and bent down to perform his lifesaving duty.

As they tiptoed backward out of the lounge bar, they heard Signora Strega-Borgia yell, "Get a *move* on. Send an ambulance, a helicopter, whatever you can. This man is *dying* and you're doing nothing to help."

They closed the door behind them. Damp's eyes were round pools of terror. Seeing Dada hitting the smelly man and then *kiss* him was so outside Damp's range of experience that she involuntarily slipped into the chorus of Grade Three.

"Hush, hush, there, now," soothed Mrs. McLachlan, carrying the whimpering baby into the residents' lounge and sinking into an armchair by the fireplace. "It's all right, pet. Daddy and Mummy are a bit too busy right now to help us find your big brother and sister, so we'll just have to manage by ourselves."

Ten minutes later, somber-faced and giving the thumbs-down signal behind Damp's back, Latch entered the lounge. At a loss for words, he pulled his dressing gown tighter round his lanky body and busied himself with trying to revive the fire. "Awful business," he muttered. "And there's no sign of those children. I've tried the kitchen, had a quick check round the pool—I even tried the stable block, but. . . ."

"They'll have gone back to StregaSchloss," said Mrs. McLachlan grimly. "Despite being expressly forbidden to do so. I *thought* something was going on this evening—did you notice how preoccupied they were over dinner?"

"To be honest, no," admitted Latch. "I was more concerned with why my wardrobe door was broken, why the floor was covered in wee things like rabbit droppings—and, talking of droppings, the beasts are on the loose."

"I beg your pardon?" Mrs. McLachlan stared at the butler.

"I kid you not—there's a tunnel dug through the stable-block floor, and not a trace of them to be seen. Plus—and *this* one completely defies understanding—I seem to have lost every single pair of socks that I possess, all the towels have disappeared, and I can't find my toenail clippers anywhere. . . ."

"What in heaven's name have socks and toenail clippers got to do with StregaSchloss? And where have those beasts gone?" sighed Mrs. McLachlan. "I think we're going to have to find Titus and Pandora for the answer. I'm going to dress the baby and myself and you call a taxi. We're going to StregaSchloss."

Thinking wistfully of his warm bed, Latch heaved a sigh. Maybe there was a simple explanation that didn't involve heading out into a December night. Maybe the children had decided to give the beasts a pedicure and take them for a walk? Maybe they'd been breeding rabbits in the wardrobe? Latch's frown deepened. His imagination failed him totally when it came to the missing socks. Eleven pairs? What on earth could Titus want with them? And the broken door—what of that? With a furrowed brow, Latch followed Mrs. McLachlan upstairs.

The Road Less Traveled

In their tropically overheated living room, Vincent Bella-Vista and Vadette were having a row. On the glass-topped table separating them, a pile of Styrofoam beefburger cartons, overflowing ashtrays, and toppled beer cans bore witness to an evening of overindulgence that had rendered the builder and his girlfriend bloated, tipsy, and spoiling for a fight.

Pausing in her attempt to remove her engagement ring and hurl it across the room at her fiancé, Vadette was struck by a thought: "THISH ISHN'T EVEN A DESHENT RING!" she bawled, lowering her voice to a sob. "Jusht a poxshy wee ring for your poxshy wee girlfriend—eh, Vinnie?" Beyond reason and consumed by drunken outrage, she hauled herself to her feet and lurched through to the kitchen, continuing over her shoulder, "And I know where I'll find a *proper* diamond, shince you're too cheap to buy me one. . . ."

"You wouldn't know a proper diamond if it bit you on the bum," Vinnie muttered, lighting his forty-seventh cigarette of the evening and dropping its smoldering predecessor in his empty beer can.

"I'm talking about the diamond you told me about—I'm going to find the one in the chandelier at ShtregaSchloshhh," said Vadette, her words accompanied by the crashing sound of cupboards being opened and slammed shut again.

"StregaSchloss? Now? You want to go out there right now? It's . . ." Vincent gazed in disbelief at his watch.

"Yesh. I *know* it'sh three o'clock. I'm going to help myshelf to a deshent diamond." Vadette raked through the cutlery drawer till she found what she was looking for.

With a disgusted snort, Vincent Bella-Vista dragged himself out of his chair and stomped into the kitchen. In the pitiless fluorescent lighting Vadette looked like a demented doughboy. Furthermore, she was brandishing a rolling pin in a distinctly threatening fashion.

"Aww, come on, Vadette." Vincent took a step backward. "You'll never find that diamond in a million years, even if it does exist. There are thousands of crystals in that chandelier. . . ."

"I'm going to shmash it to pieshes," Vadette declared. "*That* way I'll find the diamond, cosh real diamonds don't shmash."

There was a perverted logic to this, Vincent realized, watching as Vadette grabbed her coat and van keys and staggered out of the front door. The vision of her descending on StregaSchloss intent on an orgy of drunken violence was too horrible to contemplate, and he called after her retreating form, "Look. Can't we talk about this? I'll *buy* you a proper diamond.

I'm going to make so much money on this deal that I promise I'll find you one as big as the Koh i noor ”

His words were cut off in a roar from an engine, as Vadette gunned the accelerator and took off down the drive in her van.

Carrying bramble thorns sheared from the bushes with the aid of Latch's toenail clippers, the clones were now armed and dangerous. Intent on following Beelzebub and exacting their revenge, they emerged from the thicket and assembled in the middle of the track leading to StregaSchloss. Twin circles of light heading in their direction failed to alert them to the dangers of loitering in the middle of a highway. The clones simply did not have the experience to understand what approaching headlights signified. Dazzled, blinded, and dimly aware that this might not be A Good Thing, they turned to face the source of light. Gravel peppered the roadside as a taxi bearing Mrs. McLachlan, Latch, and Damp swept past on its way to StregaSchloss.

In the ensuing dust and blood and chaos, the clones reeled, horrified by yet another attempt to consign them to oblivion. What use were bramble thorns against such a vast enemy? But, just as they turned the thorns of their entanglement into weapons for their defense, they conceived a plan to turn the dazzling gravel demon into something they could use to their advantage in the pursuit of Beelzebub. When the next set of headlights appeared in the distance, they were ready. Their plan took nerves of steel. It involved a lot of hitching up of socks round waists, of bunching ponchos under armpits to free up their limbs. Closer now, headlights bouncing as the gravel demon negotiated the pockmarked track. The clones tensed and held their thorns pointed outward. . . .

As Vadette drove past in the white van, the clones leapt forward. With a howl composed in equal parts of terror and effort, they flung themselves onto the spinning rubber rims of the tires. With a massed scream, they clung wailing to their thorns as they spun, over and over, round and round, in a dizzying, thundering orbit, their tiny knuckles bone white with the supreme effort of hanging on.

Gagged, bound, and bundled into the dungeon at StregaSchloss at gunpoint, Titus and Pandora had never been so frightened in their lives. After what felt like hours spent weeping in the darkness of the dungeon, they heard a taxi pull up, then the sound of footsteps crossing the rose quartz, and for one glorious moment, hearing the voices of their nanny and butler, they thought that rescue was at hand. Overhead, filtering down to the dungeon and echoing off its dank stone walls, came the welcome voice of Mrs. McLachlan inquiring as to their whereabouts.

"Oh, heavens, no . . . ," said Mrs. Fforbes-Campbell. "How *awful*. Vanished, have they? I don't think they'd be stupid enough to come here—we haven't seen them at all, have we, Hugh?"

"Children?" said the roofing contractor, rolling the word around his mouth with the kind of disdain normally used for words like "cockroaches." He waved his arm around, indicating the great hall surrounding them. "I hope they wouldn't be so misguided as to come here. . . . Far too dangerous. . . . This house could collapse at any time." Seeing the blank expression of Mrs. McLachlan's face, he elaborated, "Just got here ourselves. Ffion here gave me a lift, since my car was destroyed by your dragon thing."

"Do you make a habit of going out at three a.m. to check on the progress of your contracts?" Latch peered suspiciously into the sepulchral gloom of the great hall, turning back to Mrs. McLachlan for support. The nanny had unzipped Damp's snowsuit and was engrossed in checking the status of the baby's diaper. Damp submitted wearily to this indignity.

"Oh, Damp, not now. . . . Excuse us for one moment . . . ," Mrs. McLachlan said, sweeping past Mrs. Fforbes-Campbell and opening the door into the tiny downstairs bathroom. She slammed the door behind her, locked it, placed the unjustly accused Damp on the floor, and, to the baby's continuing mystification, took her powder compact out of her bag and flipped it open.

"Is that *another* car?" said Latch, unwisely turning his back on Hugh Pylum-Haight and crossing the hall to look out of the door. "What *is* going on?"

Behind him, the roofer exchanged a meaningful look with his partner-in-crime, pulled a walking stick out of a rack in the coat stand, and brought it down with an audible crack on Latch's head. The butler staggered back from the front door and collapsed on the floor.

A nearby flushing sound signaled the imminent return of Mrs. McLachlan and Damp. Behind the bathroom door, Mrs. McLachlan snapped the i'mat shut and shuddered. In the swirling face powder and tiny mirror, she'd seen enough to know that they were all in immediate danger. Plucking Damp off the floor, she hugged the baby and considered what to do next.

"Go and check on those awful children, would you?" whispered Hugh Pylum-Haight. "And hurry up—we've got company. . . ."

Through the hall window, he saw the lights of Vadette's white van swing across the drive. Huddled in her mink coat, clutching her crocodile-skin handbag, Mrs. Fforbes-Campbell ran along the corridor to the kitchen, carefully picked her way across the floor, and, in the feeble light from her flashlight, negotiated the slippery steps that led downstairs to the dungeons.

Vadette drew up outside StregaSchloss and parked at the front door. As soon as the vehicle stopped, the intrepid clones, all of whom had managed to hang on to their thorns, crumpled onto the rose-quartz gravel. Their simultaneous withdrawal of three hundred and eighty-two thorns caused all four tires on the van to collapse like deflated balloons. All thoughts of clone revenge had vanished in their short and brutal journey. All they wanted was for their world to stop spinning. Hissing faintly, they staggered dizzily into the shelter of a bush.

Inside the van, unaware that she'd been immobilized by the clones, Vadette switched on the inside light and peered at her reflection in the rearview mirror. In her haste to get to StregaSchloss, she hadn't taken the time to apply any makeup. Being the kind of woman who would have bemoaned the loss of her lipstick as her lifeboat pulled away from the sinking *Titanic,* she rooted in her handbag and found an old tube of scarlet lipstick. She'd just applied the first coat of this when a voice in her ear whispered, "Oh, dear me, no. I *don't* think so. Has anyone ever told you that particular shade of red makes you look ten years older?"

Vadette's hand jerked, scrawling a line of red across her cheek as she searched in vain for the source of the voice.

"Try mine," it advised. "So much more flattering to the aging complexion—and, believe me, *I* should know."

Vadette's heart hammered in her chest as a lipstick-wielding hairy leg appeared in her peripheral vision. "AUGHHH! A SPIDER!" she shrieked, attempting to beat Tarantella back with her handbag. Mumbling incoherently, "Spiders . . . aughhh, help, help . . . ," Vadette toppled sideways and slid under the steering wheel in a faint.

The air was freezing in the dungeons. Water dripped down the walls, mist wove itself round the deserted beasts' cages, and Ffion Fforbes-Campbell drew the collar of her fur coat round her neck with a shiver. The beam of her flashlight picked out a familiar shape huddled in a far corner. There they were, the Strega-Borgia brats, still tied up where she'd left them. . . . The flashlight fell with a clatter to the floor, its wildly swinging beam picking out the stuff of which nightmares were made. In a state of wide-eyed terror, unable for one frozen moment to move or even scream, Ffion Fforbes-Campbell dragged her gaze up from where Titus's and Pandora's feet were chained to rusting iron rings set in the mossy flagstones of the floor. Her eyes trawled onward, past the children's bodies, roped and bound to the bars of Ffup's old cage, over their hands, which waved and twitched in a parody of greeting, and up, up to the worst horror of all. For yes, the Borgia brats were still there, just as she'd left them, with the notable exception of their heads. Titus and Pandora were . . . headless.

Her state of frozen disbelief shattered as Ffion Fforbes-Campbell opened her mouth and screamed blue murder.

Hugh Pylum-Haight was becoming distinctly twitchy, waiting upstairs in the complete silence of the great hall. Outside, Vadette's van was parked in the drive. Its headlights had gone off and its interior light had gone on, but when Hugh looked outside, there appeared to be no one at the wheel. Furthermore, the nanny and baby *still* hadn't emerged from the bathroom, despite his demands that they do so. With the situation rapidly slipping out of his control, Hugh Pylum-Haight decided to act. Banging once more on the bathroom door, he yelled, "OUT! Come on. I know you're in there. Out, or I'll shoot."

Silence greeted him. His own words echoed in the vast stillness of StregaSchloss. There was not a sound from downstairs, utter silence from the partly lit van, not a squeak from the bathroom, and finally, when Ffion Fforbes-Campbell's shrieks came howling up from the depths, Hugh Pylum-Haight lost what little nerve he had. Firing three times at the bathroom door, he bolted down the corridor to the dungeons.

Outside, waiting in the kitchen garden, the beasts took the three gunshots as their cue for action. Tock slid into the moat to guard his lily pad larder, Sab flew up to the roof to keep a lookout, Knot shuffled bravely into the kitchen, and Ffup excused herself with a pressing need for a pee in the parsley bed.

Hugh found Ffion Fforbes-Campbell backing up the dungeon stairs, gibbering incoherently. "HUGHHH . . . there's something *awful*—just horrible happened down there. . . . We *have* to get out. . . . Those kids . . . No heads . . . There must be something down there—run, RUN!" She threw herself at the roofer, propelling him backward.

The dim light filtering down on them from the kitchen was suddenly blotted out by an enormous shadow. "OH, MY GOD!" Ffion Fforbes-Campbell screamed. "It's *here*. BEHIND YOU!"

Hugh Pylum-Haight was knocked aside by something vast—something that stank to high heaven and mumbled to itself as it reached out to wrap the mink-draped Mrs. Fforbes-Campbell in its woolly arms.

Totally unnerved, Pylum-Haight fled for safety. Stumbling up the stairs, he found himself in the kitchen. A bitter wind blew through the open door leading to the kitchen garden, and across the floor a trail of muddy footprints led to the dungeons. Echoing up from their depths, a series of slobbering gobbling sounds seemed to indicate that Ffion would not be following behind him. Cravenly, Hugh Pylum-Haight decided to take her Land Rover and escape by road.

Outside in the kitchen garden, Ffup was still squatting over the parsley, sighing mightily and hoping that her quick bathroom stop might relieve the strange feeling in her tummy. The dragon stood up, dabbing ineffectually at her bottom with what appeared, in the darkness, to be a small towel. Nope, that hasn't done the trick, tummy still feels weird, thought Ffup, groaning miserably. She couldn't work out what was wrong with her. She'd been feeling ravenous, off and on, all night, but now she just felt nauseous. Rubbing her tender stomach, she turned toward the house.

A figure bolted out of the kitchen and ran headlong into the dragon, its head making painful contact with Ffup's abdomen. There was a shriek, a lethal blast of dragon flame, and Ffup ran screaming into the house. In the kitchen garden, drenched in dragon pee, the hapless towel-clad clone that Ffup had mistaken for toilet paper crept closer to the incinerated and still smoldering remains of Hugh Pylum-Haight and attempted to dry herself in the warmth.

"Ambulance! *Help!* I've crisped somebody!" wailed Ffup, skidding across the kitchen and into the corridor. The stench of burning roofer clung nauseatingly to her nostrils. "Urghhh, I'm going to be si—" Ffup hauled open the door to the downstairs bathroom, failing to notice the three bullet holes, or the fact that she'd wrenched the door off its hinges in her efforts to obtain access. Just in time, the dragon managed to get her head down the toilet and immediately emptied her insulted stomach of its cargo of half-digested seaweed and a few lumps of mutton.

Wedged overhead, her feet against one wall, her back against another, with Damp cradled asleep across her lap, Mrs. McLachlan tutted. "What *have* you been eating? Och, you poor wee pet. . . ."

Startled to hear herself addressed by such a sympathetic toilet, Ffup banged her head on the cistern as she peered upward. Mrs. McLachlan beamed down at her from the ceiling and pressed a warning finger to her lips.

On the other side of the ruined door, a voice complained, "Run this past me again. You hurl your engagement ring at me, call me a cheapskate, and run off into the night armed with a rolling pin. I follow you. . . . Halfway here an insane cat falls through my windscreen, claws me to ribbons. . . . I finally make it here to find your motor's got four flat tires, you're out cold on the floor, I have to climb over a body to get in the front door, and all *you* can go on about is a spider with lipstick. Just tell me, in words of one syllable, what the devil is going on."

Another voice, female this time, replied testily, "Aw, shut up,

Vinnie. Let's just go back home. Forget I ever mentioned diamonds. This place gives me the creeps."

"Not till I've found Huey," came the rejoinder. "I know he's here somewhere. I can smell that poncy aftershave he's always wearing. My guess is he's out on the roof checking out the damage. If *you* can't tell me what's going on, then maybe *he* can. I want an explanation. . . ."

The sound of footsteps going upstairs faded away into silence. Mrs. McLachlan slid down the walls till she came to rest beside Ffup. With a stern warning to guard Damp with her life, she passed the sleeping baby across to the dragon and headed off to try and find Titus and Pandora. The dragon looked down on her slumbering charge. Strange maternal feelings stirred beneath the scales of her breast. Patting Damp gently and tucking the baby deeper under her wing, Ffup settled down on the bathroom floor to wait for Mrs. McLachlan's return.

Halfway down the dungeon stairs, Knot lay curled in a massive hairy ball, his hands folded across his distended stomach. He'd devoured Mrs. Fforbes-Campbell in three vast gulps, without pausing to chew between mouthfuls. With his appetite temporarily satisfied, the yeti had fallen into a fitful belching slumber. A few uneaten clumps of Ffion's mink coat dotted the stairs around him, and a crocodile-skin handbag was propped up behind the yeti's head.

Mrs. McLachlan edged past his inert form and descended into darkness. Grunts and squeaks alerted her to the children's whereabouts. Stumbling in the gloom, she caught sight of them eerily lit by Ffion Fforbes-Campbell's abandoned flashlight. Mrs. McLachlan blinked a couple of times and then strode forward, totally unfazed by their headless state.

"Very funny," she muttered, untying the knots that bound them. "Just tell me what you think you're both doing here in the middle of the night. If your parents knew about this little escapade, they'd have a fit. . . ."

Titus reached up to where his head should have been and produced a soggy rolled-up handkerchief out of thin air. The effect of this was most peculiar. Untainted by vanishing cream, his mouth suddenly appeared, its seeming lack of connection to anything resembling a face producing the weird image of lips waving in space. Beside him, Pandora's mouth appeared likewise.

"It was *her,*" moaned Titus. "Her and her precious spider and rats."

"Oh, *right*. We're not mentioning *your* clones, are we?" snapped Pandora.

"Clones?" said Mrs. McLachlan. "Just what exactly have you two been up to?"

Both disembodied mouths snapped shut.

Mrs. McLachlan frowned. "Frankly, I'd far rather be tucked up in my nice warm bed than down here freezing to death in the company of several murderous villains, four escapee beasts, and a pair of ungrateful children who haven't the sense to do as they're told—"

From overhead came the sound of a colossal crash. Mrs. McLachlan's eyes widened in alarm. Remembering the nanny's dire warnings about the perilous state of StregaSchloss, Pandora began to cry. "It's going to collapse . . . ," she wailed. "We'll be buried alive!"

"QUICK!" yelled Titus, grabbing the flashlight. "There's a way out by the moat. Down the sewage tunnel along here—hurry up, we can't hang around here waiting for the walls to come down."

As if to emphasize the urgency of his words, another crash echoed and reverberated round the dungeon. Trusting that Ffup had enough sense to take Damp and Latch outside to safety, Mrs. McLachlan followed the children down the labyrinthine passages that linked the dungeons to the moat.

Beastly Confessions

Perched on one of the exposed roof timbers like a living gargoyle, Sab was giving himself a severe talking to. *That* had just been too clumsy for words. Most un-griffin-like behavior. Should be deeply ashamed of yourself. He looked at his curved talons, turning them this way and that and tutting as he did so. What a complete numpty, he chided himself, even though he'd just been trying to help. A few minutes ago, the griffin had come across Vincent Bella-Vista and Vadette, picking their way across a particularly dodgy section of roof, and offered them a helping talon. . . .

Digging those same talons into the roof timber to keep himself from accidentally slipping off into space, Sab looked down through the open heart of StregaSchloss. A vast hole appeared to have been blasted through it from roof to cellar. Splintered wood and shattered plaster still rained down through the hole, pattering and crashing through floors and ceilings, and coming to rest in a pile on the distant floor of the great hall—a pile of timber and rubble under which lay two still figures, their blood leaching out across the floor beneath.

"I can't apologize enough," whispered the griffin. "So sorry. But you shouldn't have put up such a struggle. I was only trying to help. . . . This roof is so dangerous, and there you were, clambering around on it. And then—well, I'm just *gutted*, frankly. That'll teach me to leave well enough alone. . . ."

With a flap of his leathery wings, Sab glided off his perch and arrowed down, down through the house, through a rising cloud of plaster dust, down to the great hall, where he landed, skidded inelegantly on his slippy talons, and, recovering his balance, came to a standstill beside Latch.

"Um . . . ," said the griffin, prodding the butler's inert form, "could you wake up and talk to me? Please? I think I've done something awful. . . ."

"Me, too," said Ffup, emerging from the bathroom with Damp still asleep in the cradle of her wings.

"Well, *I* don't feel in the least bit guilty," said Knot, appearing at the end of the corridor. "She was *deeelicious*."

Latch's eyes fluttered open as he tried to focus on the beasts bending over him, their eyes moist with concern.

"We've got something to tell you . . . ," began Ffup.

"You're going to be awfully vexed," Sab said, his voice tinged with regret.

"Are you *sure* you know where we're going?" Mrs. McLachlan's voice betrayed no sense of the terror she was desperately trying to conceal from the children as she followed them blindly along the tunnels beneath StregaSchloss.

"Er . . . yes," Titus lied, pausing to lean against the wall and wait for the other two to catch up. His back ached horribly from the crouching gait they'd had to adopt as the roof of the tunnel gradually began to slope down toward the floor. Mrs. McLachlan was completely hunched over, walking like a bear, her hands groping along the floor, feeling for her way in the dim light from Titus's flashlight.

The air in the tunnels was stale and chill, smelling of damp and decay. At one point they'd crossed a fetid puddle: Mrs. McLachlan recognized the reek—it was the recently flushed contents of the downstairs toilet intermingled with other horrors too gruesome to relate. She had wisely kept this information to herself as the children gagged and choked up ahead. Stranded in the shallows were several soggy envelopes and a long, drenched snake of toilet paper. Remembering the long-ago morning when Damp had flushed the post down the toilet, Mrs. McLachlan shuddered in disgust and transferred the soggy envelopes to her breast pocket, a kind of talisman against their return from the tunnels—and also in case they contained anything of importance to the family.

Pandora staggered over to where Titus crouched, waiting for her, and slumped onto the wet floor with a small wail. "We're going to die, Titus," she said bleakly. "We'll never find our way out. In hundreds of years they'll find our shriveled remains, and we'll end up in a museum labeled THE BOG DWELLERS OF ARGYLL." She closed her eyes and groaned. "I'm so tired. I feel like we've been walking down here for miles and miles. I just wish—" She stopped abruptly in mid-sentence, opened her eyes, and grabbed Titus's arm. "What's that?"

The rhythmic *splash splash* of Mrs. McLachlan's crawling

echoed behind them, the sound overlaid now by a quieter pattering noise.

"It sounds like rain," murmured Titus, peering up ahead into the darkness.

"Can't be," said Mrs. McLachlan, coming to a halt beside Pandora. "Not down here."

Titus's flashlight picked out something moving in the distance. "Oh, *no . . .* ," he groaned. "That's all we need. Disgusting. It's a *rat*."

Mrs. McLachlan forced herself not to scream. She'd almost grown used to Pandora's pet rats, but wild subterranean ones were a different matter entirely. . . .

"Oh, *yes*!" yelled Pandora, clambering over Titus in her haste. "Don't you see? It's not *a* rat, it's *my* rat! Oh, Titus, we're going to be all right—it's Multitudina!"

Up ahead, Multitudina skidded to a standstill. Doesn't *smell* like her, she decided, blinking as the dancing girl bore down on her. Sounds familiar, though. What on earth is my trained biped doing down here? Further speculation was curtailed as Pandora scooped Multitudina up in her arms and rained kisses down on her head.

"Euchh. Look at its *teeth*," Titus gagged. "Yellow fangy things. Pandora, you're *weird*. Don't kiss—oh, yeurchh, tell me I'm not related to her."

Titus and Mrs. McLachlan waited, shuddering with a mixture of cold and disgust as, in between kisses, Pandora explained why they were currently touring StregaSchloss's dungeons.

Finally losing patience with his sister's kiss fest, Titus

interrupted. "Listen, Multitudina, if you can lead us out of here, I'll personally empty the contents of the freezer onto the floor and you can eat the lot. That's a promise."

Needing no further encouragement, the rat wriggled out of Pandora's arms and swam off down the tunnel. She paused to check that the bipeds were following, squeaked her approval, and set off once more.

Splashing behind in Multitudina's wake, Titus, Pandora, and Mrs. McLachlan followed their unlikely savior along the tunnel to freedom.

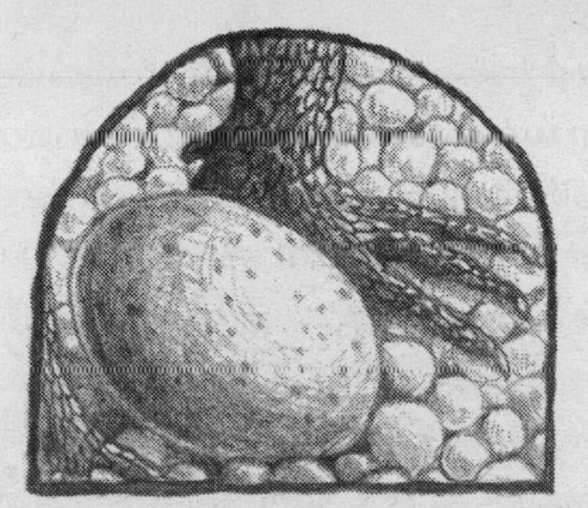

Stone Skimming

Plaster dust filled the air as Latch, Tock, and the beasts sat round the kitchen table drinking tea and devouring an overlooked packet of digestive biscuits. Washing the milk jug out in the sink, Knot had found what he'd taken to be a small and tantalizingly rancid fur ball glued to the bottom of the jug. He'd been about to devour this when the fur ball informed him that its name was Terminus and proceeded to put up such a fight that the yeti had been forced to hurl it, squeaking, into the kitchen garden. Deeply puzzled, Knot helped himself to another biscuit and scratched his bottom thoughtfully.

Oblivious to all the drama, Damp slept on Ffup's lap, her chest rising and falling in time with her little snores. The butler had stoked the kitchen range, and now it clanked and bubbled in the background, throwing out heat all around the room.

"So"—Latch was attempting to grasp the details of what had

passed while he'd been unconscious on the hall floor—"what is needed here is for us to come up with some convincing way of making it look like all four of those deceased criminals met with an accident when they broke into StregaSchloss."

"Shouldn't be too hard," said Sab, pouring himself another cup of tea.

"But we've got three vehicles and only two corpses," Latch reminded the beasts. "Knot's eaten the third and Ffup's toasted her partner. How are we going to explain the extra car?"

"If we could dispose of the Land Rover, who's to say they were even here? Apart from ourselves, no one knows that they came to StregaSchloss tonight." Ffup rubbed her tummy and groaned deeply. "We'd have to get rid of the crocodile-skin handbag, but Tock could give it another state funeral. . . ."

"But the car," insisted Latch, "we can't bury a car."

"We could push it in the loch, with the barbecued roofer in it," suggested Sab, "or—even better—Ffup and I could fly with it out to the middle of the loch and drop it in. No one knows how deep it is out there."

"But the taxi driver," said Latch, "he took Mrs. McLachlan, Damp, and me out to StregaSchloss. He's a witness. . . . Oh, this is all so hideously complicated."

"I'm in no fit state to carry a car plus a roofer out to the middle of the loch," moaned Ffup. "My tummy hurts."

Sab lost patience. "The alternative is admitting that you turned an innocent citizen into a charred heap of carbon—I think the police might take a rather dim view of such unprovoked behavior. . . ."

"All right, all *right*." Ffup stood up. "Come on. Let's do it. First the car, then the handbag."

The beasts and Tock followed, obliterating all incriminating tire tracks as Latch drove the Fforbes-Campbell Land Rover down to the loch shore. On the seat beside him, smoldering gently, Hugh Pylum-Haight's remains still emitted a faint but recognizable whiff of aftershave. Latch turned the engine off and climbed out onto the pebble beach, gently taking Damp from Ffup's cradle of wings.

With a deep sigh, Ffup attempted to hoist the vehicle onto her shoulders. "Oofff—it's heavier than I thought. . . . Maybe this isn't such a good idea."

"You're such a wimp," Sab complained, gripping his side of the Land Rover and swinging it upward with a grunt. "Stop moaning and get on with it. If you hadn't toasted that bloke, we wouldn't be doing this."

Groaning and squabbling, the dragon and the griffin effortfully climbed into the sky, their wings laboring as they bore the weight of the vehicle and its cargo between them. Slowly they flapped out across Lochnagargoyle, the Land Rover's wheels barely cresting the little waves that splashed back to shore, where the others watched anxiously. Damp woke up in Latch's arms and gazed calmly around. Since flying cars are the everyday currency of infant picture books, the bizarre sight of a Land Rover winging its way across the loch barely caused her to frown. Surrounded by her familiar beasts and lulled by the sound of the waves breaking on the beach, she sighed and went back to sleep.

Out over the uncharted deeps of the loch, the dragon and the griffin nodded to each other. On a count of three they let go. Making hardly a splash, the Land Rover slipped beneath the surface, sinking rapidly to the bottom of Lochnagargoyle and leaving no trace of its passing. Relieved of their burden, Ffup and Sab flew back to the shore and joined their co-conspirators.

"What an effort," moaned Ffup. "Hang on a minute—I need a poo."

"What, *again*?" said Sab. "You've really got a problem with your tripes, pal. This is the tenth time tonight."

Ignoring this, Ffup squatted on the pebbly beach in full view of her horrified companions.

"Oh, *please,*" groaned Sab, pointedly turning his back and picking up a skimming stone. "At least have the decency to go behind a bush." He selected a perfect skimming stone, totally flat and utterly square, and drew back his paw in preparation for throwing it.

"Wait a minute . . . *stop*! Don't do that!" Latch made a grab for Sab's paw.

Behind them, Ffup shrieked, "I *can't* stop! OW! OW! OWWW! It HURTS!"

"Not you, you daft dragon—*him*. Sab, let me see that stone." Latch prised Sab's talons apart and examined the skimming stone.

"It's not a *stone*! It's a BOULDER!" Ffup screamed. "AAARGH! I'm going to BURST! HELLLLP!"

Tock ambled over to where Ffup squatted. The dragon's eyeballs were bulging with effort, tears rolling down her long nose. Little puffs of steam came from her nostrils as she heaved and strained over the pebbles.

"You need a laxative," the crocodile said helpfully. "Should have eaten more fruit. Prunes and apricots—that sort of thing. . . ."

The dragon panted faster and faster, her little breaths punctuated with the occasional snort of flame.

"Sab—where did you find this stone?" said Latch, hardly daring to believe what he was holding.

"That one?" said the griffin. "Oh, it was one of the ones Tock found for me earlier this evening—when we were playing around after we'd eaten the sheep. There's *millions* of them in the water. Ask Tock—he'll get you more. D'you want a game? I warn you, I'm a world-class stone skimmer. . . ."

"AUGHHH urgh AUGHHH!"

"Relax," muttered Tock. "Now push. Go for it."

"RRRGH urgh MMMNG."

"*Well done!* Take a break. Relax."

"It's a *slate*!" cried Latch. "It's a StregaSchloss roof slate!"

"Don't be silly," said Ffup, waddling back to the lochside with Tock beaming beside her. "It's an *egg*. My very first one. Look, everyone! I'm a mummy!"

In her claws, the dragon held a blue speckled egg, not unlike a vast rugby ball. Ffup glowed, she twinkled, and she looked so proud and radiantly happy that everyone clustered around her, all thoughts of slates and roofs temporarily forgotten as they laughed and hugged each other, passing the egg around carefully as they absorbed the miracle that had occurred in their midst.

Down to Business

Multitudina reached the edge of the moat and dragged herself onto comparatively dry land. Behind her, gasping with the shock of swimming in such icy water, came Mrs. McLachlan, with Pandora towing Titus behind her.

"Time you learned to swim," Pandora said, crawling out of the water and turning to haul a dripping and choking Titus onto the rose quartz beside her. Above them, the stars shone clearly in the icy chill of the winter's night. Stumbling and shivering uncontrollably, heedless of StregaSchloss's structural dangers, they ran in through the front door, praying that Damp, Latch, Tarantella, Tock, and the beasts had not only survived, but had kept the home fires burning.

In the kitchen, the beasts and Latch rose to greet them. Damp slept, tucked into a bed hastily improvised from a cutlery drawer, swaddled in tea towels, and utterly oblivious of the events surrounding her. In the absence of a roof over her attic,

Tarantella was spinning herself a temporary web in the china cupboard. The beasts had been sitting round the kitchen table, cooing and exclaiming over Ffup's egg, but with the arrival of the drenched party from the dungeons, they lurched into action. Latch rushed upstairs to find dry towels and changes of clothing and Sab put the kettle on. Feeling distinctly overlooked, Multitudina sulked under the table as Pandora, Titus, and Mrs. McLachlan admired the egg.

"Oh, it's absolutely *beautiful*!" exclaimed Pandora, not daring to touch it in case her shivering hands let it slip. "Aren't you clever? It's magnificent, Ffup! When will it hatch? Oh, I can't wait . . . A baby dragon . . ."

"I assume it *is* a dragon, dear?" said Mrs. McLachlan, peering suspiciously at the egg cradled in Ffup's lap.

The proud mother smiled beatifically and pretended she hadn't heard the last question. Knot ambled over to the range, scratching his tummy and emitting a pungent reek of rancid mutton combined with the perfume of old dog. Catching a whiff of this foul odor, and reminded abruptly of Titus's rancid goose incubator, Pandora choked and moved out of olfactory range. This made her the first thing the clones caught sight of as, unannounced, they herded into the kitchen in search of comfort.

"MAMAAAA!" they bawled in unison, running toward her, tiny arms outstretched, tripping pathetically over their socks and ponchos in their headlong rush.

"Oh, *no*!" squeaked Pandora. "*No way!* Not *me*, you numpties, I'm never going to be a mothe—"

Swarming over and past Pandora, the clones threw

themselves onto the bewildered Knot, clambering up his filthy fur, snuffling ecstatically at his faintly remembered stench, his pungent smell of fetid meat. It was a smell that spoke to the clones of their brief babyhood, of their early days in the goose incubator, and so it was hardly surprising that they assumed Knot to be their mother. Pandora watched in horror as the clones buried themselves in the yeti's unhygienic nooks and crannies, sobbing and whimpering as they did so.

"WAUGHHH HELLLLP!" wailed the yeti, overwhelmed by the vast numbers of clones currently taking gross liberties with his person. With his entire body covered in wriggling figures, Knot panicked, stumbled, and, with a desolate shriek, fell over onto Ffup's lap. The egg bounced under the impact, rolled down Ffup's leg, and trundled rapidly across the floor, headed for the kitchen garden. It wobbled perilously on the edge of the step, seemingly intent on ovisuicide, and then appeared to undergo a change of heart. In full view of everyone it stopped, appeared to levitate itself to a handspan above the doormat, and retraced its path back across the floor.

From the kitchen garden came the clearly audible command, "Left. Right. Left. Right. HAAAAAALT! After three, down to the floor. STEADY! Don't DROP it, whatever you do. . . . One, two, three, DOWN! Fifth Battalion of the Dragon's-Tooth Engineers, AT EEEASE!"

The egg was gently lowered to the kitchen floor, and, to the astonishment of the onlookers, out from under it marched a dozen tiny men in kilts.

"Oh, my heavens . . . ," whispered Titus. "The Dragon's-Tooth Tincture! Mum'll *murder* me if she finds out."

"What? What are you on about?" Pandora picked up one of

the tiny squaddies and examined him. He tried to hide under his shield and, failing in the attempt, braced himself for extinction.

"Mum had a bottle of Dragon's-Tooth Tincture in the fridge, as part of her homework from the Advanced Witchcraft Institute," Titus explained, "sort of an instant army kind of thing. Add water and stir, and ten minutes later you're overrun with squaddies."

"But they're *teeny,*" said Pandora, peering under the kilt of one she held prisoner in her hand. He battered her feebly with his shield in an effort to preserve his dignity.

"Your mother used Ffup's baby teeth to distill the tincture," said Mrs. McLachlan. "*That* might account for their size. . . ."

Pandora returned the indignant squaddie to the company of his battalion. "We're becoming overrun with wee things without pants," she said. "First Titus's clones, now these animated toy soldiers, not to mention Ffup's egg."

"Excuse *me,*" snorted Ffup, plucking her egg off the floor and tucking it protectively under one wing. "It may not be wearing any underwear, but my *egg* is not vertically challenged."

"No one said it was, dear," said Mrs. McLachlan soothingly. "It's a very fine egg, and I'm sure one day it will grow up to be a great strapping dragon."

"*That* would be highly unlikely," muttered Ffup under her breath, returning to her seat by the range.

"But what are we going to *do* with them all?" wailed Titus.

Latch came through the kitchen door carrying a pile of towels and clothes. Mrs. McLachlan and Pandora helped themselves to some of these and disappeared into the privacy of the pantry to change. The butler's jaw dropped as he absorbed the sight of milling squaddies and wriggling clones. "What on earth is going on?" he demanded, dropping the remaining towels at his feet.

The clones instantly abandoned their surrogate Knot parent and leapt at the new sartorial opportunities represented by such a mountain of toweling. Recognizing several of his stolen socks running across the kitchen floor, Latch turned to Titus for an explanation.

"Ah, yes . . . er . . ." Titus grabbed Multitudina from under the table and sidled off in the direction of the pantry. "Back in two ticks. I just have to honor a promise I made to Mul . . . Mult . . . um, yes . . ."

Latch groaned and sat down at the table. Sab appeared at his elbow with a cup of tea and leant over to pat him with a consoling talon. "Drink up," the griffin murmured. "It'll all seem so much better in the morning. . . ."

"It *is* the morning." Latch gazed at his watch for confirmation. "Soon I'll have to telephone my employers and explain that we are all here, at StregaSchloss, and not tucked up in our beds in the Auchenlochtermuchty Arms. Also, I will have to present Signor and Signora Strega-Borgia with the happy news that not only is their missing roof lying at the bottom of Lochnagargoyle, but—oh, joy—they have hundreds of extra mouths to feed. Then there is the little matter of a massive hole driven through their house by flying criminals and, lest I forget, the fact that their staff and children have been party to four murders, killing the only chap who could have repaired the damage to the roof in the first place. . . ."

"But at least we've found the missing slates," said Sab, determinedly clinging to the positive aspects of the night's events.

"Oh, aye, in the loch—they're about as much use as chocolate teapots, aren't they?" Latch replaced his teacup in its saucer and sighed.

"But don't you *see*?" Sab grabbed the butler's arm, causing his teacup to slop its contents across the table. "With the slates we can fix the roof!"

Dabbing at the puddle of tea in front of him, Latch took a deep breath. "Much as I hate to be a killjoy—if you recall, Ffup *crisped* the roofing contractor. The roof is falling to bits. . . . I doubt if you'd find a replacement firm of roofers who'd be willing to risk life and limb up there, crawling over the trusses, trying to nail tiles onto wood that might not bear their weight. . . ." Depressed beyond belief by his own gloomy predictions, Latch closed his eyes and laid his head on the table with a groan.

However, Sab was not to be deflected from his mission to bring good cheer to the butler. "Look, here's my plan. Tock gets the slates back out of the loch and we'll organize the tincture squaddies to put them back on the roof. Heaven knows, there's enough squaddies to do the job, and being so tiny, they weigh hardly anything. The rest of the damage to the inside of StregaSchloss can wait."

Taking Latch's silence for assent, Sab assembled his troops. "Right, Tock, let's go. Back to the lochside. We need to pick the slates up and bring them back here. Ffup, you sort the squaddies out, would you? Since they originally came from your teeth, they ought to obey you without question. . . ."

In the wine cellar, Titus took a deep breath to steel himself for the task ahead and opened the lid to the freezer. At his feet, Multitudina meditatively nibbled on the corner of a frozen fish finger. True to the promise he'd made in the dungeons, Titus had emptied the freezer of a box of fish fingers, a brace of game pies, several tubs of ice cream, and twenty or so assorted unlabeled bags of leftovers. Now he peered into the freezer, where Strega-Nonna lay enshrined in tinfoil, her silver hair forming a frosty corona around her little walnut-wrinkled face. Strega-Nonna was the most ancient resident at StregaSchloss, her history forever entwined with that of the house itself, her encyclopedic knowledge making her the family's living archive. On several occasions, she had been known to defrost herself and arrive unannounced in their midst, an anachronistic reminder of their eventual wrinkly fate. Unable to let go her hold on life, even the half-life of the cryogenically preserved, she clung on determinedly, at first suspended in icebergs, then kept in the old ice house on the grounds of StregaSchloss, and finally, with the advent of domestic refrigeration, entombed in the deep freeze, hoping that one day science would find a cure for old age.

Titus's breath formed misty clouds around her as she gazed up at him. "Nonna . . . ," he began, "how d'you fancy some company in there?"

Strega-Nonna sighed. Company? She considered this. It had been centuries since she'd entertained any form of company worth considering. "What did you have in mind, child?" She shifted her weight and pulled out a bag of frozen peas from under her arm and passed them out to Titus.

"Three hundred and eighty-two very small geriatrics," Titus said, dropping the peas near Multitudina. "Or, at least, they look like geriatrics, even if they're only three days old."

"How small?" said Strega-Nonna. "There isn't all that much room in here."

"Tiny. No bigger than your hand. And there's heaps of space now that I've removed all the food."

"Right now?" Strega-Nonna said, considering this possibility. "I'll have to tidy this place up a bit, dust, vacuum, that sort of thing. . . ."

"So, is that a yes?"

"I'll give it a go," said Strega-Nonna. "But I reserve the right to evict them if things don't work out. Now shut the lid, child. I'm beginning to thaw. . . ."

Titus closed the freezer lid and groaned. Time to explain to Mrs. McLachlan exactly where the clones had come from, and take her advice on whether to phone Signor and Signora Strega-Borgia or let them sleep on in blissful ignorance. And, Titus reminded himself, he really ought to apologize to Latch for using his socks as a rudimentary form of clone clothing. He turned toward the kitchen, where he found Pandora and Mrs. McLachlan devouring the remnants of a packet of digestive biscuits with a freshly made pot of tea.

The nanny met Titus's eye, waved her hand in the direction of several clones sleeping in little heaps round the kitchen, and raised one eyebrow inquiringly. While Latch snored with his head on the table, Titus began to explain what on earth had possessed him to think that cloning himself and his sister was A Good Idea. Somehow, in the soporific warmth of the kitchen, the nightmarish quality of the whole clone episode seemed far away, like a bad dream. Mrs. McLachlan murmured sympathetically, the rewound clock over the mantelpiece measured out the minutes, Damp lay tucked snugly under a mound of tea towels in the cutlery drawer, and Ffup's egg took pride of place, set in a copper jelly pan, hung on a hook over the range.

During a pause in Titus's narrative, they all heard the clatter of a vehicle coming round the back of the house. Outside the kitchen window, Vincent Bella-Vista's van lurched to a standstill and Knot, his fur alive with clones, fell out of the driver's door onto the rose quartz. The passenger door opened and Sab emerged, shaking from head to tail.

"I'll do the driving next time, pal," he advised. "I thought we were going to *die* back there."

"I can't see what I'm doing," Knot complained, brushing clones away from his eyes. "It's all these wee *things*. They're all over me—eurchhh, get *off*!"

The unwanted clones gathered their socks and ponchos about themselves and headed indoors for warmth.

"FFUP!" bawled Sab. "Here's the first batch of slates. Come and get them." The griffin turned and opened the van's rear doors and began to remove slates from its interior and stack them on the driveway.

Ffup swooped down the south face of StregaSchloss to the rapturous applause of the entire battalion of tincture squaddies, lifted a hundredweight of slates in her talons, and flew back up more sedately to where the squaddies waited to begin work on the roof. Leaving the remaining slates to be airlifted roofward, Sab and Knot climbed back in the van and headed down to the loch for more. Despite the now continual hammering from the roof, Mrs. McLachlan, Titus, and Pandora joined the sleepers in the kitchen, twitching and snoring in the warmth from the range. The racket of the arriving and departing builder's van failed to wake them as Knot and Sab brought twelve more loads of slates back to StregaSchloss, finally returning just before dawn with Tock shivering and dripping as he clung to the roof rack.

Deep-Frozen Dollies

A faint pink glow could just be seen over the treetops when Damp woke up. During the night, several clones had crawled into the cutlery drawer beside her, and were now curled round her legs, eyes tight shut, their faint whispery breath barely audible.

Funny dollies, Damp decided, prodding one to see how it worked.

The Pandora type opened its eyes and gave a disgruntled hiss. "What a *night*," it groaned, to Damp's delight. "Eeeeh, I'm stiff. Must be the arthritis. . . ." And off it staggered, clambering painfully over the edge of the cutlery drawer and groaning pitifully as it hobbled across the floor. Mystified, Damp crawled out of the drawer and followed the escaped dolly over to where it halted at the range, using the coal bucket as a mirror and bemoaning the state of its gray hair, which was coming out in handfuls.

Broken dolly, Damp thought with regret, Nanny fix it. She padded across to where Mrs. McLachlan slept on the settle and crawled into her lap.

Overhead, the banging and hammering ceased. The change in background noise level served as a trigger to wake everyone up. Before removing themselves to the Auchenlochtermuchty Arms, the family had stored all their mattresses in the bed attic, their linen in the linen cupboard, and every pillow that had ever graced the beds in StregaSchloss had been sent away for re-covering and cleaning. Consequently, sleeping in the warmth of the kitchen rather than in their bare and arctic bedrooms had seemed like a good idea at the time, but now, stiff and sore after a night spent on hard chairs, Mrs. McLachlan and Latch were not inclined to be cheerful.

"Where are those pestilential beasts?" muttered Latch, opening the range and riddling the ashes within. Lifting the mirror-gazing clone to one side, he emptied the contents of the coal bucket into the firebox and slammed the range door shut with a kick. "I'm going to the coal shed. Would someone please put the kettle on for some coffee?"

His clattering and banging woke the clones. They were dotted here and there around the kitchen, some in drawers, some camped in mixing bowls, some draped across chairs, and even one sock-clad Pandora type hanging from a cup hook in the china cupboard. They groaned and wheezed in concert, alerting Titus to their parlous state.

"They've grown *old*," he said, realizing that their gray hair was due not to a lack of personal hygiene, but to a case of accelerated aging. "Oh, the poor things, how *awful*."

Pandora rescued the clone beside the range and sat with it in her hands, patting its head as if affection alone could turn back the clock. Titus watched aghast as his once bouncy and lithe creations stooped and hobbled around the kitchen, sharing the ghastly details of their current decrepitude with everyone within earshot.

Titus tried to shut his ears but it proved impossible.

"Gout in my toes—ohh, the agony. Can't hardly walk with the pain. . . ."

"I think I'm coming down with a chest infection—can't breathe properly."

"You should moan, I can't see with these cataracts."

"Influenza . . . might even be pneumonia. . . ."

"On the other hand, might be a touch of emphysema, or maybe bronchitis. . . ."

On and on they droned, each vying with the next in its catalogue of ailments, with Titus growing more suicidal at each new revelation. "Oh, what have I done?" he wailed, racked with guilt about the true cost of his dabblings in bio-engineering.

Mrs. McLachlan paused en route to the bathroom with Damp in her arms. "It's a hard lesson you're learning, laddie," she said, wrapping her arm around Titus and giving him a hug. "To watch those we love grow old and frail is part of life itself—it prepares us for the fate that we all inherit. . . . It's just that you're a wee bit young to have to face such things. You're still at the stage where you're determined *never* to grow old. . . ."

Damp reached out and patted Titus on the cheek. Titus leaking, she decided, batting tears off his nose with a chubby fist.

"By the time it's your turn," Mrs. McLachlan continued, "you'll realize that old age isn't half as bad as you thought. In fact, believe it or not, you'll look back to when you were a laddie and think, 'Thank heavens I'll *never* have to be twelve ever again.' It's not *all* doom and gloom, you know. Old age has its compensations. . . ." She bore Damp off upstairs, leaving Titus and Pandora to their thoughts.

Latch came back from the coal shed, his frosty breath forming clouds at the back door. "Come and see this!" he cried. "You'll never believe what's happened!" Titus followed the butler outside into the kitchen garden. He followed the line of Latch's pointing hand, squinting up to where he could see the roof gleaming in the early-morning light. The slates reflected the rosy blush of the sky, and on every ridge, miniature figures danced, giving each other high fives and hooting with delight. Perched on the chimneys, Sab and Ffup watched the caperings of the tincture squaddies like guardian gargoyles, occasionally scanning the horizon to see if there was anyone to witness the structural miracle that they'd managed to pull off.

"The roof!" gasped Titus. "It's back! What . . . how? Oh, this is *amazing*! Wait till Mum and Dad . . . OH, YES! We don't have to leave! WE DON'T HAVE TO LEAVE! LATCH, WE DON'T HAVE TO—"

"Eh? What's that you said?" A clone tugged at Titus's shoelaces, cupping a tiny hand to its ear to aid interpretation. "Deaf as a post, I'm afraid. Run that one past me again, m'boy?"

Titus plucked the clone off the ground and dropped a smacking kiss onto its bald head. Here was an impossible thing: a miracle. Where once was no roof, no *hope* of a roof, no home—a box in Bogginview the bleak prospect ahead of them—now, here was StregaSchloss restored to its former state, its turrets and crenellations sparkling in the sunlight. The impossible made possible, in fact. Titus kissed the bewildered clone again and carried it inside to the kitchen.

Pandora sat at the kitchen table, a tiny limp body in her hands. "He's dead, Titus," she sniffed. "He died in my arms. Clutched his wee chest, went blue and fell over. . . ." She burst into tears.

Titus knew that they had to act, now, before the remaining clones met the same fate. "Pan, you have to help me get them into the freezer with Strega-Nonna. Maybe, just maybe, there'll be a cure for old age one day. Who knows? What seems impossible today might be commonplace in the future. . . ." Seeing his sister's disbelieving glance, Titus persevered. "I have to *try*, don't I? I *made* them. I can't just write them off as a failed experiment. They're like children. *My* children. D'you think Mum and Dad would have binned us if we'd been a bit faulty?"

"You *are* a bit faulty, Titus," sniffed Pandora with a rapid return to her normal sibling lippiness. "Personally, I would've taken you back to the hospital you were born in and asked for a refund."

"That's a bit academic, isn't it?" retorted Titus. "Since you're always saying you're *never* going to have children."

"And *you're* always banging on about never growing old," said Pandora. "Now I can see why. Look at the clones that are like you. They're bald and wrinkly. Eughhh."

Squabbling to keep their thoughts away from the task at hand, Titus and Pandora gathered up all the living clones and, wrapping them in tinfoil, transferred them to the freezer. There had been a significant decrease in their numbers. Overnight, the seemingly overwhelming clone population had dwindled to a modest hundred or so little bodies. Closing the lid on Strega-Nonna's welcome speech to her new freezer mates, Titus and Pandora began the grisly cleanup operation, scouring the house and grounds for little corpses and laying them in a row next to their kin in the rose garden. With the assistance of Tock, they buried the clones under one of Signora Strega-Borgia's rosebushes and tried to maintain the necessary gravitas as Tock reverently laid Mrs. Fforbes-Campbell's crocodile-skin handbag to rest beneath a clump of saw-toothed pampas grass.

Inside, Mrs. McLachlan hung Pandora's and her own wet clothes over the range to dry. As she straightened the sleeve of her soggy blouse and draped it over the towel rail, a wad of sodden envelopes fell to the floor. Above the nanny's head, the egg wobbled in its jelly pan, and patting it absentmindedly, Mrs. McLachlan bent down to retrieve the wet post, remembering with a shiver where she'd found them, floating in a foul puddle down in the dungeons. She was still rinsing them under the kitchen tap when Titus and Pandora came in from their grave-digging duties.

"Can we phone Mum?" asked Titus, joining the nanny at the sink. "Tell her about the roof? And maybe *not* tell her much about what else happened."

"*I'll* phone," said Mrs. McLachlan, handing the dripping envelopes to Titus. "Here, take these and very carefully try to separate them. Then lay them out flat on the hot-plate lids on the range. With any luck, they might just about be legible once they're dry."

"How come they're so wet?" asked Pandora. "Did the postman not put them through the letterbox? Were they outside?"

"They date back to the beginning of December," said Titus, peering at the blurred postmark on one of the envelopes. "Couldn't we just chuck them in the bin? No one would ever know. . . . They all look really boring—bills and stuff."

"There might be something of interest in them," said Mrs. McLachlan firmly. "Or there might not. They're wet because your baby sister thinks the downstairs toilet is a sort of postbox with a disappearing handle. . . ."

"Oh, YEUCHH!" Titus regarded the pile in his hand with disgust. "I'll probably catch bubonic plague from these things."

"Titus, dear, no one is asking you to *eat* them," said Mrs. McLachlan, opening the door to the great hall. "Just sort them out, wash your hands, and look after Damp for a moment. I'm going to make a few phone calls."

Shutting the door behind her, Mrs. McLachlan headed for the telephone in the great hall. Shivering in the echoing space, she prepared what she was going to say as she dialed a number. Sunlight streamed through the stained-glass windows on the landing, illuminating the pile of plaster and broken beams that entombed the bodies of Vincent Bella-Vista and his girlfriend, Vadette.

On the other end of the telephone, someone picked up, and clearing her throat, Mrs. McLachlan began, "Good morning, Sergeant, Flora McLachlan here at StregaSchloss." That much was true—but as to the rest—she crossed her fingers tightly. "I'd like to report a break-in. . . ."

Going Home

The Scottish flag on the roof of the Auchenlochtermuchty Arms drooped forlornly, and inside the hotel the staff went about their daily routine in hushed silence. The atmosphere was subdued, as all staff and guests waited to hear how Mortimer fared. After the proprietor's sudden collapse and subsequent departure to hospital by air ambulance, Signor and Signora Strega-Borgia fell into their bed, stunned by the wickedness of what they had discovered.

"It was *her,* Luciano. That awful Ffion woman. I knew she was dangerous from the moment we met her." Signora Strega-Borgia lay wide-eyed and wakeful, oblivious to the rosy dawn breaking outside their bedroom window.

"The paramedic was certain that he'd taken poison," said Signor Strega-Borgia, aghast at such marital perfidy. "To think that she's lived and worked beside the poor old beggar, and every day she was spiking his nightcaps with rat poison, just watching and waiting for him to die. . . ." He turned to his wife for reassurance. "You would never do a thing like that, would you, Baci? No matter how much you wanted to be rid of me?"

Signora Strega-Borgia turned to face her husband and wrapped her arms round him. "Oh, I don't know . . . ," she said, trying hard not to laugh. "My cooking's undoubtedly bad enough to kill you ten times over, but not *intentionally,* you understand."

"Don't joke about it." Signor Strega-Borgia's voice came out muffled by his wife's embrace.

"I'm not," she replied. "Look, I promise you if you ever drive me so mad that I want to get rid of you, I won't be so devious as to use poison. Okay? I'll just buy a gun and shoot you instead."

"That's fine," said Signor Strega-Borgia. "Since your aim is as appalling as your cooking, I can safely look forward to a long and happy life."

The sky was full of light when the telephone rang downstairs in reception and was automatically transferred through to the hotel kitchens, where a number of staff were preparing breakfast for early-rising guests. The short-order chef expertly flipped a trio of fried eggs with his spatula and then hurtled across the kitchen to answer the telephone.

"Aye? Auchenlochtermuchty Arms. Four-star accommodation in the heart of Argyll. How can I help youse?"

The voice on the other end had to shout to be heard over the sound of spluttering eggs and bacon.

"Dunno. Dinnae think he's up yet. Shall I find out?" The chef punched a couple of buttons on the phone and watched disgustedly as his eggs blackened round the edges. At last there came a reply on the other end of the phone. "Took yer time, didn't youse?" he bawled. "There's a phone call in reception. D'youse want it in your room or are youse going to come doon here for it?"

On the other end of the telephone, Signor Strega-Borgia yawned copiously. Thirty minutes' sleep had left him neither refreshed nor in full possession of his faculties. He looked across the bed to where his wife lay slumbering sweetly beside him. Shame to wake her, really.

"Come oan," growled the chef. "Ma eggs are ruint. Make up your mind, youse."

"I'll come down," Signor Strega-Borgia decided, replacing the receiver on the chef's wrath, grabbing a dressing gown, and tiptoeing out the door.

Five minutes later, he was back, wide awake, and hauling his protesting wife out of bed. "Come *on,* Baci. Get dressed. That was the police on the phone. We have to go to StregaSchloss."

"But I'm *exhausted* . . . ," his wife groaned, hauling herself upright and attempting to bring her eyes into focus. "Luciano, please. . . ."

Signor Strega-Borgia was hurling clothes out of their wardrobe onto the bed. "Hurry up. They'll be here in five minutes."

"Not the purple organza, darling, I'll *freeze*."

"Wear a pullover, then. Come *on*. That's the police car now."

Signor Strega-Borgia looked outside and saw a black-and-white car sweeping up the drive to the hotel. Behind him, muttering as she threw on clothes, jumpers, scarves, two pashminas, and a serape for good measure, Signora Strega-Borgia cursed as she dressed for the Scottish winter. Red-eyed from lack of sleep, clumsy and crumpled, the couple ran downstairs to where their escort awaited, the car's blue flashing light lending an air of drama to the scene.

"If you'll just step into the rear of the vehicle, sir, madam." A burly policeman stood holding the rear door open for the Strega-Borgias. They obediently slid into the rear seat, and without a second's delay, the car shot off along the drive in a shower of disturbed gravel, siren on and blue light still flashing.

Signor Strega-Borgia leaned forward to address the back of the necks of the two policemen in front of him. "Is all this really necessary, Constable?" he said. "All this fuss? Blue lights, sirens, and whatnot?"

"It's *Sergeant* MacAllister, sir," said the left-hand neck, without turning round. "We've received a phone call from a Mrs. Flora McLachlan regarding a break-in—"

A crackle from the radio interrupted him. "Delta Umbrella Mango Bravo Oscar, do you read me, over?"

Sergeant MacAllister cleared his throat and replied, "I read you loud and clear, Bravo Oscar Sugar Sugar."

"How quaintly affectionate . . . ," observed Signora Strega-Borgia.

"Query present whereabouts, over."

"Heading for incident near Lochnagargoyle on the B80261, proceeding in a westerly direction, over."

The driver of the police car, who was not involved in the radio discussion, turned round to face Signor and Signora Strega-Borgia with a wide smile. This did nothing to increase the Strega-Borgias' confidence in the police, since they were currently bouncing down the track to StregaSchloss at an indecent speed. "Just like television, isn't it?" he remarked, turning his attention back to the road just in time to avoid hitting a tree. "Builds public confidence, this sort of thing. We can't just be seen to putter round the Highlands like Police Constable Plod. . . ."

The car swerved round a tight bend, splattering mud and pebbles in all directions. Signora Strega-Borgia lurched against her husband as the car shrieked to a stop at the gate to StregaSchloss.

"That's them!" yelled Sab, positioned as lookout on the topmost turret. He saw a figure emerge from the car to open the gate a quarter of a mile down the track. In the kitchen, Mrs. McLachlan and the children waited. Latch stood in the great hall, ready to open the door. The beasts clung to their turrets and chimneys, attempting to look as gargoyle-like as possible. In the moat, Tock swam to the edge to greet his beloved mistress.

Stepping onto the rose-quartz drive, Signora Strega-Borgia swathed herself in shawls and looked around. Shading her eyes from the sun, she craned her neck backward to regard the wreckage of the StregaSchloss roof, mentally steeling herself not to burst into tears at its terminal condition. Her shawls fell to the ground, her mouth fell open, and for a few seconds she forgot to breathe. Above her, the roof shone in the morning light.

"The roof! The *roof*! The *house*! Oh, I don't *believe* it! Yes, I do! OH, MY HEAVENS! IT'S LIKE MAGIC. . . ." She turned round, face alight, and dragged her husband out of the police car.

Signor Strega-Borgia, still half-asleep, squinted up at the apparent miracle of restoration. He blinked rapidly, rubbed his eyes, and threw his arms round his wife. "Baci?" His voice came out in a squeak. "Am I awake? Our house? Am I seeing things? If this is a dream, *please* don't wake me. . . ." Picking Signora Strega-Borgia up in his arms, he spun her round in circles on the rose quartz, laughing hysterically. "OH, WE'RE HOME! HOME! HOME!"

The front door opened to reveal Latch, pale and drawn. "Welcome home, Signor, Signora. . . . So sorry that you had to return to this . . . ," he murmured, wringing his hands. "Terrible business . . . poor people—obviously didn't read the sign outside. . . ."

Utterly confused by this somber greeting, the Strega-Borgias followed the butler inside and beheld the pile of wood and rubble that had formed a partial tomb for Vincent Bella-Vista and his unfortunate girlfriend. Powdered with plaster dust, their faces glowed eerily through the fallen debris.

"Oh, *dear,*" said Signora Strega-Borgia. "The *poor* things. . . ." She looked upward, up through the vast hole above the wreckage, the ragged edges of which stretched up through the darkness, all the way to the newly repaired attic. She dragged her gaze downward with a shudder to the two corpses. "But . . . that's Mr. Belle Atavista . . . and his girlfriend. I wonder what on earth happened to *them*?"

Skirting the pile of wreckage, the police sergeant stepped

into the great hall and, removing his notebook from a pocket, flipped it open. Judging by their performance on the doorstep, he'd already come to the conclusion that Mr. and Mrs. Strega-Borgia were, in all probability, utterly insane, but he had to follow police procedure. . . . With a deep sigh, he began: "Were you acquainted with the deceased? Sir? Madam?"

"Both the sir and the madam," said Signor Strega-Borgia, averting his eyes with a shudder from the gaze of the builder sprawled under the pile of broken timbers. His eyes met those of Latch, and he realized that the butler was drawing his finger across his lips in a mime of "Keep quiet." His thoughts in chaos, Signor Strega-Borgia stammered, "He . . . um . . . Mr. Bella-Vista . . . was about to . . . was about to . . . yes, he was about, round and about in the . . . um . . . hotel." He risked a glance at Latch, to see if this blundering improvisation had met with the butler's approval.

Unaware of the signals passing between Signor Strega-Borgia and Latch, the policeman carried on. "And when was the last time you saw either of the deceased alive?"

"Yesterday afternoon," said Signor Strega-Borgia. "He drove us back to the hotel after we'd been to Bog—after we'd been . . . um . . . out to see his . . . DOG! Yes, that's right, his dog. . . ."

Signora Strega-Borgia interrupted her husband. "Sergeant, none of this explains *why* we were told that our house had been destroyed. Two of your constables, in fact, told us that this house was in such a parlous condition that we'd be risking life and limb to return."

The sergeant harrumphed, licked his pencil nervously, and avoided Signora Strega-Borgia's eyes.

Twitching a shawl impatiently round her shoulders, she

continued, "Yet, Sergeant, here we are, *in* the property, apparently in no danger whatsoever, apart from the odd falling builder, and outside are notices—*police* notices—to the effect that StregaSchloss is extremely dangerous."

"There appears to have been some confusion about this matter, madam." The policeman was now looking distinctly nervous. "Officers Macbeth and McDuff will be suspended from duty pending a full inquiry."

"You admit that there has been a mistake?" said Signor Strega-Borgia, stepping forward.

"Um. Yes. No. I mean, I'm afraid I'm not able to comment on that." The policeman was clearly floundering now, shuffling his feet and casting despairing glances in the direction of the front door.

"But, look here, Sergeant, you simply can't go round misinforming innocent members of the public about the structural safety of their houses." Encouraged by Latch's wide grin, Signor Strega-Borgia was warming to his theme. "Dragging them out of their beds, forcing them to view dead bodies draped across their hallways. . . . I mean, it's hardly our fault if these two were unwise enough to fall through our attic, is it?"

He gripped his wife's arm and began to steer her in the direction of the kitchen. "Come on, Baci. I'm so sorry I hauled you out of bed on a fool's errand. Let's go and have some coffee and leave the police to deal with this mess, shall we?"

Beetroot-red with embarrassment, the policeman said, "Er, one last thing, sir, if you would be so kind? If you could just identify the bodies, I'll arrange for them to be removed as soon as possible. . . ."

Signor Strega-Borgia heaved a sigh and joined the sergeant by the pile of rubble. Both the bodies wore expressions of polite surprise, as if by plunging through several floors of rickety real estate they had committed some minor breach of etiquette.

"To the best of my knowledge, Sergeant, that one on the left is Vincent Bella-Vista, and the other is his lady friend, Vadette—I don't know her surname, as we were never properly introduced."

"They've made a right mess of your house." The policeman produced a flashlight and shined it up through the damaged ceiling.

"We'll get in touch with our roofer," said Signor Strega-Borgia. "Hugh Pylum-Haight—d'you know him?"

"Indeed we do, sir. He appears to have done a runner, I'm afraid. We're looking for both him and Mrs. Ffion Fforbes-Campbell in connection with an attempted murder."

"Good Lord," said Signor Strega-Borgia. "You mean the poor chap at the Auchenlochtermuchty Arms?"

Conscious that he'd said far too much, and learned nothing in return, the policeman snapped his notebook shut, replaced his flashlight in his pocket, and clasped his hands behind his back. "Did I hear you mention coffee?" he said, attempting an ingratiating smile. "I could *murder* a cup, myself. . . ."

"Unfortunate choice of phrase, don't you think?" murmured Signora Strega-Borgia, leading the way down the corridor to the kitchen. She pushed open the door and sniffed appreciatively. "Mmmm. Delicious. Oh, Flora, you *have* been busy. . . ."

Sitting round the kitchen table, devouring cinnamon and raisin muffins, were Titus, Pandora, and Damp. Mrs.

McLachlan, resplendent in a cook's apron and oven mitts, was just removing a trayful of chocolate fudge brownies from the oven. She straightened, pink-cheeked and beaming with pleasure. "Welcome home, dears. I knew you would be a little peckish so I've made some fruit scones, raisin muffins, fudge brownies, and praline cake, and the meringues should be ready in a minute.... Come and sit yourselves down by the range, you must be *frozen*."

Drawn by the heavenly smell of baking, the policeman edged into the kitchen behind Signor and Signora Strega-Borgia. Gazing at the fount of such culinary largesse, he caught sight of Ffup's egg, dangling in its jelly pan over the range. "What in heaven's name do you feed your chickens? That's some egg you've got there," he said in tones of reverence.

Damp slid off her seat and teetered across the floor toward her mother. A cascade of muffin crumbs tumbled in her wake as she blissfully wrapped herself round Signora Strega-Borgia's knees. Making sure that her employers were comfortably ensconced on the settle, their cups full of coffee, with Damp and a plate of brownies between them, Mrs. McLachlan turned her attention to the hovering policeman. "Some coffee, Sergeant?" she said, fetching an extra mug from the china cupboard. She filled this and passed it across to the policeman but pointedly did not press him to take either a seat or a piece of home baking. With a tut of apparent displeasure at her own appearance, Mrs. McLachlan produced her powder compact and began to dab at her nose with the powder puff. Pandora tensed when she saw this, wondering whose inner thoughts were about to be invaded by the magical i'mat. When the nanny swiveled round to point the back of her mirror at the unwitting policeman, Pandora held her breath. Was he about to arrest them all as accessories to murder? Was he even faintly suspicious? Or could it be that he was utterly unaware of what had really happened at StregaSchloss?

"There. Nothing like a wee bit of artifice," said Mrs. McLachlan, snapping the i'mat shut and dropping it into her apron pocket. "Much better, I think."

Pandora exhaled with relief and helped herself to another muffin by way of celebration. Mrs. McLachlan winked at her, the nanny's whole being radiating the knowledge that they had indeed gotten away with it. In her mirror, she had seen a vision of the policeman carrying a file labeled STREGASCHLOSS down a set of stairs into a basement. In the tiny i'mat screen, the policeman had opened a dusty filing cabinet in the darkest recesses of the basement and hurled the file inside. In the swirling face powder below the soul mirror, the words FILE UNDER "FORGET" and HATE PAPERWORK had appeared briefly.

Hence Mrs. McLachlan's broad smile, and her hospitable offer of "More coffee, Sergeant? And you *must* try some of my muffins. . . . Here, have a couple."

The Borgia Inheritance

Preparations for a Scottish Hogmanay at the Auchenlochtermuchty Arms began early in the morning of that last day of the old year. In the absence of both proprietors, the remaining staff had raided the Fforbes-Campbells' wine cellar and were applying themselves to Mortimer's cache of vintage champagne. The chefs and chambermaids gathered in the lounge bar to toast the health of their absent employers and failed to notice a taxi drawing up at the front of the hotel. Mortimer, pale and shrunken, climbed out of the rear and tottered up the steps to the entrance. Under strict instructions from the doctors at the hospital not to touch any alcohol whatsoever, he had been allowed home to celebrate the new year. He carefully negotiated the revolving door, tiptoed across the tartan carpet, and headed purposefully for the forbidden solace of his stash of Old Liverot in the laundry room.

Just one sip, he thought, and with his hands trembling at the prospect, he uncorked the bottle and raised it to his lips. "Chin, chin, Morty, old chap," he muttered. "Bally doctors don't know a thing, what? Bunch of quacks, wet behind the ears. . . ." He paused, suddenly aware of a scraping sound emanating from one of the laundry sinks next to the industrial washer-dryer.

"Rats, what?" he snorted, staggering across to peer into the sink. "If She Who Must Be Obeyed had put the blasted poison down for *them* instead of feeding it to Yours Truly . . ." The old man's eyes watered as he considered the recent attempt made on his life. "Rum old thing, marriage, what? S'posed to love, honor, and obey and all that rot, and there she was, trying to bump one orf. . . ."

Once more he raised the bottle to his mouth, but before the first sip could cross his lips, the drain cover in the sink lifted up, clattered across the porcelain, and a tiny naked figure clambered arthritically out of the open drain, wheezing and creaking as it did so. Simultaneously, the bottle of Old Liverot shattered on the laundry room floor as it fell from Mortimer's grasp.

"Much worse than I thought, what?" he mumbled. "Seeing things already. Little pink men in the laundry. Bodes ill, Morty, old bean. Time to lay off the sauce, what? No more of the cup that cheers for this chap. . . ."

Rubbing his eyes, Morty spun round and marched out of the laundry room into his future, which, from the moment he'd seen the geriatric clone exiting the drains, he'd vowed would be a tee-total one.

In the games room at StregaSchloss, several tincture squaddies were engaged in a protracted game of Monopoly while their peers snoozed, happily slung in pockets on the billiard table.

Running the full length of one wall, a glass-fronted bookcase groaned under the weight of several thousand board games beloved by generations of Strega-Borgias. Chess sets in materials as diverse as Carrara marble and lapis lazuli were stacked on top of battery-operated games of Battleship. An antique game of Go reputed to have been made for the Emperor T'ai Ph'Twang had become intermingled with the porcelain and gold tiles from a mah-jongg set dating back to the P'ing dynasty. Jigsaws, cards, roulette counters, poker chips, spillikins, marbles, yarrow stalks, dice, jacks, Trivial Pursuit wedges, bridge score-sheets, discarded Pictionary doodles, Scrabble tiles, bits of unidentifiable plastic, and shards of Bakelite, wood, and metal formed a jumbled compost capable of engaging a dedicated housekeeper for several months of full-time sifting, cataloguing, and sorting into the correct boxes. In between looking after Damp and producing ovenfuls of delicious food, Mrs. McLachlan would spend approximately one hour each week attempting to tidy up the mess, but so far had made little impression.

Wishing that she could find herself a Mrs. McLachlan clone to sort out the chaos in the games room, Signora Strega-Borgia opened the door and sighed deeply. She reminded herself that being a householder in the sprawling pile of ninety-six rooms that comprised the interior of StregaSchloss meant that any attempts to impose order were forever doomed to failure, and picked her way across the room to gaze out of the window that afforded the best view of Lochnagargoyle. Behind her back, the tincture squaddies dotted across the billiard table attempted to look as much like inanimate tin soldiers as possible, considering they were all dressed in kilts.

"Happy, darling?" Signor Strega-Borgia crossed the room to join his wife where she stood framed by the spectacular view beyond her.

"Blissfully, Luciano," she said, indicating the vista through the window. "I'm so glad to be home—and just in time for fireworks at midnight. . . ."

Together they looked down to the loch shore, where Latch was hammering large wooden stakes into the pebbly beach, watched by the beasts and Tock. On the jetty, three wooden crates were stacked one on top of the other, their combined contents comprising enough gunpowder to ensure that this new year would be welcomed in with an assault on the eardrums that would render the residents of StregaSchloss totally cloth-eared for hours afterward.

In the far distance, a hearse bore the bodies of Vincent and Vadette back to the village for burial. Sergeant MacAllister's car followed at a respectful distance, a tray of Mrs. McLachlan's home baking strapped onto the back seat to ensure that the night shift at the Auchenlochtermuchty police station would not suffer a calorie famine in the wee small hours of Hogmanay.

"What do you think *really* happened?" asked Signora Strega-Borgia, watching as the two vehicles bounced down the bramble-lined track leading to the village.

"To Vincent and Vadette?" said Signor Strega-Borgia, nibbling his index finger as he considered the question. "You mean, did they fall or were they . . . um . . . assisted? Were they in cahoots with Mrs. Fforbes-Campbell and Mr. Pylum-Haight? Or, could it be that they were merely having an innocent stroll through our attic last night when the ancient timbers gave way beneath them? I suspect that Latch and Mrs. McLachlan know the answer to these questions, but in truth, I think I would rather remain in blissful ignorance. As to how our roof miraculously reappeared—well, Baci, my dearest, you've always taught me never to examine the hows, whys, and wherefores of good magic, so I'll just give silent thanks for the fact that we are all back here, safe in StregaSchloss. . . ."

Downstairs, in the kitchen, Titus was sorting through the range-dried salvaged post, while Pandora and Damp shared spatula scrapings from Mrs. McLachlan's pavlova mix.

"Two for you, Mrs. McLachlan, four brown ones for Mum and Dad, Latch's copy of the *Gentleman's Gentleman* quarterly, a postcard for Damp from . . . Oh, *dear,* Marie Bain. I'd better read it to you, Damp, shall I? Let me see. . . . Oh, heck, she's coming back . . . had a lovely holiday . . . slowly recovering from gastroenteritis . . . looking forward to being our cook again. . . ." Titus's stomach gave a warning groan in unhappy anticipation of the return of the worst cook in the Western Hemisphere. With a heartfelt sigh, he returned to the pile of mail. "Nothing for you, Pan, and . . . Hang on, this one's for me." Amazed because he so rarely received any mail whatsoever, Titus examined his envelope.

"That'll be the lunatic asylum informing you it's time to return for treatment," said Pandora, scraping the last few atoms of pavlova from the mixing bowl and offering them on a spatula to Damp. "Or maybe it's the Federation of Feebleminded Friends reminding you that your annual subscription is due. . . ."

Ignoring this, Titus opened his envelope and withdrew a single sheet of creamy laid paper, which, due to the quality of its weave, had survived prolonged immersion in raw sewage and subsequent laundering and drying on the range.

". . . or perhaps it's your plastic surgeon letting you know that he has a slot in March for your total face reconstruction," continued Pandora, peering over Titus's shoulder to read the letter. "Who on earth are Dombi, Figlio, and Sonny, W. S.? And is your middle name *really* Andronicus? Phew—what a mouthful: Titus Andronicus Chimera di Carne Strega-Borgia. . . ." Her voice trailed off as she read the next paragraph of the letter held in her brother's trembling hands.

"Er, Mrs. McLachlan, how many lire are there in a pound?" said Titus, trying to sound unconcerned, but uncomfortably aware that his voice was coming out as a shrill squeak.

"It's *ounces,* not lire, child," said Mrs. McLachlan, immersed in a recipe book. "Why do you need to know?"

"Because he's just inherited one hundred and forty-seven billion of them," said Pandora. "Or at least he will, on his next birthday."

"That's very nice, dear," said Mrs. McLachlan distractedly.

"Why did Grandfather Borgia leave all his lire to *you*?" muttered Pandora. "That's *so* unfair."

"Brains and good looks, I guess . . . ," murmured Titus. "And now money, too. Some guys have all the luck."

"Still," said Pandora hopefully, "maybe you won't make it to your thirteenth birthday. Some awful accident might befall you, and as your next of kin, Damp and I will inherit the lot. . . ."

"Your next of kin have curly tails and a tendency to say

'oink' a lot," said Titus, peering into the empty mixing bowl in dismay.

"Children! *Enough!*" said Mrs. McLachlan, looking up from her cookery book with a sigh. "Put that carving knife *down,* Pandora, and stop *gloating,* Titus. There are more important things to think about than money, you know. Now, I need your help to decide: shall I bake a pound cake or perhaps some millionaire's shortbread? What do you think?"

After Midnight

"Not 'Oh,' 'Ahhh,' 'Eek,' " sighed Tarantella, tapping her newly woven web with one of her legs. "Pay attention. Now, after me, 'O is for Orange. . . .' "

"Don't *like* oranges," muttered Multitudina.

"A is for?"

"Anything I can eat, except oranges."

"E is for?" Tarantella glared at her pupil.

"*Enything* I can eat. I've already *told* you."

Tarantella groaned. Teaching Multitudina the Illiterat to read was proving to be an uphill struggle. For the past hour, the tarantula had been weaving an alpha-web in a corner of the china cupboard. Written in spider silk were the five vowels, dotted here and there with flies that had blundered fatally into the web during Tarantella's efforts to instill the rudiments of language into her reluctant pupil. The tarantula decided to make one more attempt and then call it a day.

"I is for?"

"I hate oranges," replied Multitudina, ignoring Tarantella's moan of despair and launching herself out of the china cupboard onto the laden kitchen table. "Can't we do B instead?" she pleaded. "Look, they've left stacks of Brownies, Black Bun, Banana loaf, and . . ." She paused to deliver her final thrust: "They Bribed me to Baby-sit. . . ."

Assembled on the chilly loch shore, the family waited for the hands on Mrs. McLachlan's watch to reach midnight, signaling in the new year. Behind them, the meadow was a dark mass, out of which soared the moonlit silhouette of StregaSchloss, its turrets and tiles restored, the copper star on the observatory roof mimicking the thousand pinpoints of distant constellations that peppered the night sky. Lit by flaming torches, the family raised their glasses to the future, whatever it might bring.

"I could, of course, buy an ice-cream factory . . . ," mused Titus.

"Oh, do shut up," groaned Pandora.

"Or a private jet. . . ."

"Mum . . . he's gloating again," said Pandora.

"One minute to go," said Mrs. McLachlan, peering at her watch. Latch stepped forward and applied a smoldering taper to the fuse of the first firework.

"Then again, if you were nice to me, I *might* buy you a proper bicycle. . . ."

"*Now* you're talking," said Pandora, linking arms with Titus. "I've always wanted a mountain bike, actually . . . with an optional five hundred cc engine for those tedious uphill bits."

"Twenty seconds . . . ," said Mrs. McLachlan.

Signor and Signora Strega-Borgia hugged Damp between them, pulling her little woolly hat over her ears to muffle the impending din from the fireworks. The beasts and Tock, their eyes pools of light reflected from the torches, huddled closer to their beloved owners and bickered quietly.

"Why aren't you back at the house with your egg?" nagged Sab, digging Ffup in the ribs with a curved talon.

"Don't be *silly,*" said the dragon. "I hired Multitudina to baby-sit. I'm a teenage dragon, remember? A party animal!"

"Ten . . . nine . . . eight . . ."

All eyes were drawn to the hissing red line of lit fuse as it inched ever upward, closer and closer to the crate containing the first firework.

"FOUR . . . THREE . . . TWO . . . ," they chanted in unison.

On the stroke of midnight, accompanied by a vast boom from the loch shore, the jelly pan over the range quivered ominously. As Multitudina sat on her haunches on the laden kitchen table, her whiskers twitched. The slab of Black Bun that she'd been about to sink her fangs into fell untasted to the floor as she swiveled round to face the fireplace.

"Oh, my whiskery heavens!" she gasped in awe. "This was definitely *not* in the baby-sitting contract. Oh, my word! OH! AHHH! EEK!"

An exasperated "*Tchhhhh*" came from the china cupboard but went unnoticed as the jelly pan clattered against the mantelpiece and shards of discarded eggshell began to fall like brittle snow onto the kitchen floor.

"Gosh, um . . . yes . . . ah . . . help yourself," Multitudina whispered, indicating the tableful of delights awaiting the post-firework revelers, and, leaping to the floor, she headed for the safety of the dungeons, calling behind herself, "Be my guest . . . whatever you are. . . ."

The hatchling qualified as the most unusual newborn ever to appear at StregaSchloss. It scrabbled down the side of the jelly pan, flapped onto the floor, and crawled up a table leg in search of nourishment. On the tabletop it found a veritable feast laid out in welcome. By way of thanks to its absent hosts, the creature emitted a strangled sound halfway between a howl and an operatic high C. Glass preserve jars exploded, china mixing bowls cracked, and a pane of glass shattered in the window over the sink. With an ease that Damp would have envied, the creature slitted its eyes, drew a deep breath, and tried again. This time the priceless chandelier in the great hall shattered in an explosion of crystal, proving, as it did so, that all stories about the legendary Borgia Diamond were fact, not fiction. On the floor of the great hall, a gem the size of a quail's egg rolled out from the wreckage of the chandelier and came to rest in the untouched dust beneath the shrouded grandfather clock.

The creature paused, abashed at having vandalized its newfound nest, then with a shrug, it dipped its head and crammed a handful of sticky chocolate brownies into its mouth. Their intense sweetness coupled with the creature's complete lack of teeth caused its next howl to come out as a muffled shriek, accompanied by a shower of brownie crumbs. It gulped rapidly and cleared its palate by the simple expedient of draining an adjacent punch bowl. Clearing its throat, it threw back its head and howled loudly—so loudly that a rackful of bottles in the wine cellar exploded, showering Strega-Nonna's freezer in vintage champagne.

There, *that* was more like it. Volume, that's the thing.

From the distant hills surrounding Lochnagargoyle came an answering howl: the plaintive greeting of a legendary Scottish monster that had lived on its own for too many centuries, a mournful refrain that echoed across the meadow and bounced off the east wing of StregaSchloss. Again it came, masked by the sound of fireworks from the shore, but clearer now and more confident—a howl that sounded like a question: "Are you there? Hello? Hello?"

In the kitchen, in between mouthfuls of Black Bun, Ffup's hatchling answered: "Yes, here I am. Hello? Hello?" And, a little later, "Dad???"

They all agreed that the last firework had been absolutely the best one ever. Even Damp had emerged from the cocoon of her parents' arms to squeal as it exploded in a bouquet of vast dandelion heads made of white shooting stars that breached the night sky, their luminous tails streaking for an eternity across the loch. Deafened and dazzled, the party made its way sleepily back to StregaSchloss, unaware that the first of the new year's surprises was already there, waiting, in the kitchen.

Don't miss the next adventure of the
Strega-Borgia clan in

Pure Dead
BRILLIANT

For a sneak peek, turn the page. . . .

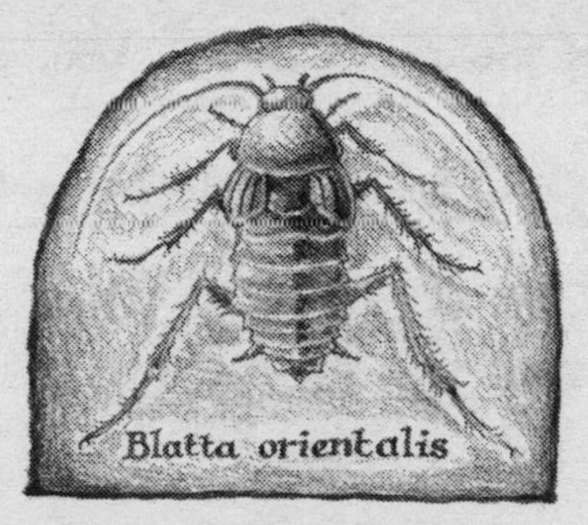

Kiss of Death

Titus decided that if there were a button to press that would cause his sister to reincarnate as a cockroach, he would push it without a moment's hesitation. He stood outside her bedroom door, seething, as he read the notice taped to the oak paneling:

PANDORA'S ROOM
entry is absolutely forbidden to any of the following:
brothers
dweebs
possessors of smelly pits & dog's breath
one-celled amoebas with memory of goldfish
smug, rich jerks
the terminally plug-ugly
the criminally insane
and *especially* the vertically challenged over 12 yrs.

Titus, all of the above describe you, so bog off.

Yours Cordially, Pandora Strega-Borgia
Pandora's Room
StregaSchloss
Argyll
Scotland
United Kingdom
Europe
Western Hemisphere
Earth
The Universe
The Galaxy

"Just because I'm about to inherit *all* Grandfather Borgia's money and you're broke doesn't mean you have to be so aggressive." Titus's voice bounced off the door and down the landing, but brought no answering response from within. He pressed his mouth up to the keyhole and tried again. "Some people just can't handle other people's good fortune, *can they, Pandora?*"

Over his head, dangling from the cornice, Pandora's pet tarantula, Tarantella, gave out an exasperated *"Tchhhh."* Titus looked up and shuddered. There was something about the scuttling nature of spiders that revolted him. This one in particular, with her swollen abdomen, gave him nightmares. Titus loathed the entire spider race with a deep and abiding passion. Their gross hairiness, their appetite for flies, their—

The tarantula grinned widely, as if reading his thoughts. "Like it?" she inquired, puckering up her lipsticked mouth parts into a pout. "It's a new one. Now, what's it called . . . ?"

Tarantella rummaged under her abdomen with one hairy leg and produced a minuscule lipstick. "Let me see . . . 'Blood-Lust.' Mmm-hmm. Come on, Titus, I know you find me irresistible, give us a kiss. . . ."

With a barely stifled shriek, Titus fled downstairs. Trembling, he burst through the kitchen door and was immediately assailed by a stench that defied description. The beasts were already at breakfast and, judging by the state of the kitchen, had been eating for several hours. Sprawled across the kitchen table, Ffup, the teenage dragon, had her vast head buried in her talons.

"Don't say it," she warned, gazing down at Titus with her vast golden eyes. "Just *don't* say it, right? I've been up *all* night with that wee horror, and now he sits there, wolfs down forty-eight Miserablios, three boxes of Ricey Krispettes, and then does a major dump, downloading the lot into his pants. I tell you, pal, I'm not cut out for this motherhood stuff. I *hate* changing diapers, and . . ." The dragon paused, peered under her baby's high chair, and whimpered, "Yup, just as I thought, it's a shovel job."

"Spare me the details," muttered Titus, edging past Ffup and patting her offending infant on his scaly little head. "Phwoarr, Nestor, you *stink,* don't you?"

The baby gazed up at Titus and grinned gummily, clapping his tiny wings above his head and lashing his snake-like tail back and forth by way of greeting. This had the unfortunate consequence of launching most of the contents of his overloaded diaper into orbit.

"Stop. Stop. STOP!" wailed Ffup. "Oh, yeurrrch. I can't handle this. . . . *Knot!* KNOT? Come *on,* help me out here."

Emerging from the pantry with a sheepish grin, Knot the

yeti shuffled across the kitchen to stare hopefully at his fellow beasts. The yeti's perpetually unsanitary fur was clotted with fetid lumps of food that had somehow failed to make the journey to his mouth. He wrinkled up his fur in the general area of his nose, sniffed deeply in sincerest appreciation of the odors in the kitchen, and sighed in happy anticipation.

"Nestor has a wee something for you," muttered Ffup, burying her nostrils in a coffee cup. "Freshly laid, still warm . . ."

"Give me strength," gagged Titus, turning his back on this revolting inter-beast exchange.

"Mmm-yummy," observed Knot, dipping an experimental paw in the puddle under Nestor's high chair. Titus moaned softly and closed his eyes. Knot sniffed, unrolled his lengthy spotted tongue, and sampled a little morsel. "Naww," he pronounced, at length. "Bit overripe, that one. Nope. Don't fancy it much."

"Don't be so picky," said Ffup. "Be a gent. Help me out. Just close your eyes and think of Gorgonzola. Pleeeeease?"

Knot wiped his paw on his tummy and scratched his armpit thoughtfully. "If you don't mind, I'll pass," he mumbled, clearly uncomfortable at the prospect of letting Ffup down. "I'm not really too hungry right this minute."

"Well, I'm *starving*," said Pandora, arriving in the kitchen by way of the door to the herb garden. "Phwoarr. Urghhh. What's that *stench*?"

"Here we go again," sighed Ffup, glaring at her baby son. "See what you've done?"

"'Morning, all." Pandora kicked off her rubber boots and came over to warm herself beside Titus at the range. "Are we all pretending that there isn't a vast pile of dragon poo on the floor over there, or is someone going to clean it up?"

"Ffup is," said Titus. "Aren't you, Ffup?"

"What? And ruin my manicured talons?" squeaked the dragon. "You can't be serious. These took me *ages*." Hoping for female sympathy, she extended one paw for Pandora's inspection. Each of her seven talons was painted a lurid sugar-pink. "Pretty, aren't they?" Ffup smirked, examining her paw with satisfaction, turning it this way and that, all the better to catch the light.

Mrs. Flora McLachlan, nanny to Titus and Pandora, entered the kitchen with their baby sister, Damp, in her arms. Smelling something truly awful and assuming that it was about to be her breakfast, the little girl buried her face in the nanny's shoulder and gave a little moan.

"Good heavens, is that the time?" Mrs. McLachlan peered at the mantelpiece clock in dismay. "My bedside clock isn't keeping very good time, and the alarm didn't go off." Then, as she became aware of the odor in the kitchen, she added, "Ffup, dear, I'm sure you're aware that Nestor needs a diaper change. D'you think you could stop admiring your manicure, stir your stumps, and do it before your mistress comes downstairs for breakfast?"

Ffup gave two snorts of flame and slowly heaved herself out of her chair. "Do I *have* to? That's so *unfair*. Why do I always have to clean up after him? It's so *boring*."

"Ffup—" said Mrs. McLachlan in a tone of voice that offered no recourse to argument.

Ffup looked up and met the nanny's eyes, which had shrunk

down to two little slits of menace. Ffup was immediately galvanized into action. "Rrright away. Where's that shovel? Rrrrubber gloves on . . . *snap.* Antibacterial spray . . . *squirt.* Scrape poo out from between flagstones on floor . . . *splat* . . ."

"The high chair, too, Ffup," said Mrs. McLachlan, one eyebrow raised.

"Yup. Yuzzm. Your wish, my command. Breathe through mouth . . . *gasp,* remove infant dragon to kitchen sink . . . *squelch,* remove diaper . . . ah. Um. Yes. Perhaps you guys might care to have breakfast somewhere else?" Ffup suggested, as her infant slid out of her grasp and landed among the unwashed dishes in the sink. "Apply gas mask . . . *urrrrgh.*"

"What have you been feeding that poor child?" demanded Mrs. McLachlan.

"Oh, *that*?" said Ffup, breathing through her mouth as she unzipped Nestor's onesie. "I couldn't be bothered to cook last night, so we just polished off the remains of a couple of boxes of chocolates and some tinned peaches in syrup we found at the back of the fridge—"

"Those weren't *peaches,*" groaned Mrs. McLachlan. "They were raw *eggs* for the cake that I was going to bake for this afternoon. Twenty-four eggs, Ffup. No wonder that poor wee mite's got an upset tummy. It's about time you faced up to the responsibilities of motherhood and grew—"

"What cake?" interrupted Titus. "Is it one of your chocolate meringue cakes? Oh, please make one of them! I'm so hungry I could eat at least six slices. Make a *huge* one. Use thirty-six eggs. Use a hundred. You're such a brilliant cook. I've never tasted cakes as good as—"

"What a crawler you are, Titus," said Pandora, regarding her brother with disgust. "Just listen to yourself. Slurp, slurp. Grovel, grovel."

"Shut up, Pan," muttered Titus. "This is for your benefit, too, you know."

"No, Titus, it's for your stomach's benefit, don't you know?" Pandora slapped her brother's midriff and tutted. "I know you're about to become a plutocrat, but there's simply no need to become a bloated one."

"Do you think, sister mine, that we might possibly, just once, let a day go by without reference to my impending vast inheritance from Grandfather Borgia? The millions that will allow me to live a life of unimaginable luxury while you, you poor thing, will only be able to watch and drool. Mind you, right now you're not so much drooling as spraying me with vitriol—I mean, anyone would think you were jealous or something. . . ."

"Oh heck, no," Pandora replied, examining her fingernails with apparent fascination. "Not in the least jealous, just a little peeved, is all. . . . After all, what possible difference could it make to me when you get your hands on your millions? It's not going to change anything important between us, is it? I mean, it's not going to make me think you're any less of a dweeb, or more intelligent, or less plug-ugly. And"—she delivered her final thrust with deadly precision—"from the moment those millions become yours, you're never, ever going to be sure if we all put up with you because you're one of us, our very own Titus, or because you're filthy rich."

Pandora turned on her heel and stalked out of the kitchen, banging the door behind her. She stormed along the corridor and across the great hall to the staircase, then took the stairs two at a time in order to reach the safe haven of her room before her feelings engulfed her. Stumbling across the moth-eaten rug, she flung herself facedown on her bed, emitting a strangled shriek. Downstairs, the grandfather clock chimed the hour, the half hour, quarter past the hour, thirteen, and then, apparently embarrassed at its own excesses, gave an asthmatic wheeze and fell silent. That was part of the problem, Pandora thought, thumping her pillow with both fists. If only she could turn the clock back and undo the past. Specifically, three months past, when Titus discovered that he was the chosen benefactor of their grandfather's vast hoard of money. Since then it was as if an invisible barrier had sprung up between her brother and herself. Everything was about to change, and probably not for the better. And yes, of course I'm jealous, thought Pandora, grinding her teeth. I'm turning a deep and unflattering shade of green at the prospect of Titus becoming a millionaire and me still having to make one measly week's pocket money last for a whole seven days.

"It's so un*fair*," Pandora wailed out loud. "Why did Grandfather leave it all to *him*?"